What the critics are saying…

Gold Star Award "Violence and mysticism – passion and love are the themes of *Sahara Kelly* in *Scars of the Lash*. … The story follows a path of twists and turns I didn't expect. I was sure that everything was going one way when *Ms. Kelly* took the story in a delightfully different direction. The interweaving of the plot of two characters in two different worlds is fantastic…a Gold Star Award story that can't be ignored by those who love books about extreme BDSM, vampires or just a heart tugging love that spans time and space!" ~ *Julie, JERR*

Five Heart Review "''…This was an awesome read! *Sahara Kelly* has outdone herself and has written a dark, violent story about a planet full of lusty, if somewhat depraved vampires. The plot is very good! It starts as a contemporary, in this time and place, then switches cleverly to another planet, another place. The reader will be pulled in on page one and the emotional roller coaster will carry the reader to heights she never dreamed of…" ~ *Valerie, Love Romances*

Five Unicorn Review "…an incredible tale of a society of warrior vampires from another world and a writer whose mind they live in…*Sahara Kelly* has mastered the written word and brought it unknowingly to its knees in submission without a fight. I fell in love with this book and I can't recommend it highly enough. It does have BDSM, yet it is done in such a way that it is totally natural in this vampire society. I am not a lover of BDSM, but with this story it's interwoven with such love and passion it's an essential element that any lover of romance would enjoy…" ~ *Lyonene, Enchanted in Romance*

Scars OF THE Lash

Sahara Kelly

ELLORA'S CAVE
ROMANTICA PUBLISHING

An Ellora's Cave Romantica Publication

www.ellorascave.com

Scars of the Lash

ISBN # 1419952560
ALL RIGHTS RESERVED.
Scars of the Lash Copyright© 2005 Sahara Kelly
Edited by: Briana St. James
Cover art by: Syneca

Electronic book Publication: March, 2005
Trade paperback Publication: September, 2005

Excerpt from *The Sun God's Woman*
Copyright © Sahara Kelly, 2002

Warning:

The following material contains graphic sexual content meant for mature readers. *Scars of the Lash* has been rated *X-treme* by a minimum of three independent reviewers.

Ellora's Cave Publishing offers three levels of Romantica™ reading entertainment: S (S-ensuous), E (E-rotic), and X (X-treme).

S-ensuous love scenes are explicit and leave nothing to the imagination.

E-rotic love scenes are explicit, leave nothing to the imagination, and are high in volume per the overall word count. In addition, some E-rated titles might contain fantasy material that some readers find objectionable, such as bondage, submission, same sex encounters, forced seductions, etc. E-rated titles are the most graphic titles we carry; it is common, for instance, for an author to use words such as "fucking", "cock", "pussy", etc., within their work of literature.

X-treme titles differ from E-rated titles only in plot premise and storyline execution. Unlike E-rated titles, stories designated with the letter X tend to contain controversial subject matter not for the faint of heart.

Also by Sahara Kelly:

Scars of the Lash

Acknowledgement

In the crazy world of a writer, ideas come from varied sources. Something as small as a song...or as large as breaking news plastered over the media. And sometimes, a very few words will be enough to begin the genesis of a story, a small spark that flames into life and engulfs the writer until it has become a fully-fledged tale.

Such was the case with this particular book. A few chance words, spoken by a friend who understands such things, and the floodgates opened to a rush of hunger, blood and the occasionally unfathomable blend of pain and pleasure. A new world formed in my head, peopled with savage strangers who would become close acquaintances, and a woman who would straddle not only the familiar, but also the strange and unearthly.

I shall forever be indebted to my Partner and friend for that chance comment. Without his words, I might never have stumbled into this universe and would have missed the excitement and challenge that writing this tale has brought me.

Part One

Sally Ann

Chapter One

"Watch, Suliana. *Watch…*" Low and commanding, the man's voice sounded in her ear.

Her hands were secured at the wrists, high above her head. Her legs were splayed wide. She was naked.

The dark purple skies were beginning to lighten as the twin moons rose, shedding a soft glow over the glade, illuminating the light mist that swirled from the dank grass beneath her feet.

Directly across from her, a woman's back gleamed softly, and her shudders and whimpers broke the stillness of the night.

"Don't look away, Suliana."

He was behind her, close behind her since she could feel his heat from her naked buttocks to the back of her neck. He was her Master. She knew this, yet fought against all that it implied.

Another crack split the air, and the woman cried out as the lash fell accurately across her ass. "No more. Wait…please…*more*."

"You love this, slut. You live for this." Another woman wiped the sweat from her eyes and bared her teeth. "Admit it." She whistled the thong of the whip through the grass and cracked it, sending the mist swirling into little tornadoes around the tip.

"Yesss…" It was a whimpered confession.

"You want to come, don't you?" His voice sounded again, distracting Suliana. "Just from watching them. You want to come."

Did she? She risked closing her eyes for a second, examining her responses.

Yes, she was aroused. Her juices were warm as they leaked from her cunt to her thighs, and her nipples were hard, beaded with arousal and ready for the taking. She knew there would be a pink flush staining her legs and buttocks. It was characteristic of her kind. Yes, she was ready to come. Ready to orgasm. She needed to orgasm. Badly.

With him.

Another whistling lash, another cry of exquisite agony, and Suliana shuddered. It should be her. She yearned for that particular pain. That crashing ascent into the place where the merest breath was torture, the most savage assault a pleasure to be savored.

Her fangs lengthened as strong arms surrounded her.

She could smell him, scent him as easily as she could scent prey when she hungered. Strong, clean, hot and spicy, his blood roused her emotions to fever pitch, much as the scene before her roused her body.

He lowered his hands, letting them rest on the front of her thighs. A hard length pressed between her buttocks, teasing her with its heat. They were joined, skin to skin, and his breath stirred the little hairs on the nape of her neck.

Slowly, he dragged his nails up her abdomen, leaving marks that would become welts in their wake. Tiny droplets of blood oozed as he marked her, filling the air around them with the sweet coppery scent of her own body's vital fluids.

"Oh yes..." She leaned into his hands, hoping he'd find her clit and drag those fingers across the hard nubbin that was straining for stimulation. She didn't care if he hurt her, in fact she hoped he would.

But he passed over her aching pussy, leaving her bereft and panting as the punishment before her continued.

"Do not despair, little flower. Your time will come." Large hands cupped her breasts. "Just watch."

Obediently, she watched. There was no choice for her. It was her destiny.

The two women writhed now, one with the whip and one beginning to bleed as she shuddered beneath each blow.

"Ah, Mayara. So sweet." The whip was tossed aside as the Domme leaned in to lick away the trails of dark maroon leaking from the lashes.

"Chanda, *please…*"

Chanda turned to Suliana, looking past her to the Master. She bared her teeth and let her fangs shine in the moonlight. "I want her. She is mine. She has asked me."

Suliana felt his head move behind her as he nodded, and she knew what his answer would be before he spoke.

"Take her. But not too far."

"Yes, Master." Chanda bent to the ground and picked up a leather device. The rubber protrusion was unmistakable in shape, and when she fixed it around her body, Suliana's cunt shuddered in anticipation.

"You are excited, Suli."

Sharp teeth nipped her ear and made her gasp, bringing her fangs out even further as she hissed her need. Did she need to answer?

No. He knew.

His fingers spread apart around her breasts, squeezing them hard, his cock a solid weight in her cleft. She squirmed, trying to find the right place, the right move to get him into her body, to ease the savage desire that was burning her from the inside out.

Sharp nails found Suliana's nipples and pinched. "Watch."

Unyielding as the chest pressed against her spine, or the cock spreading her ass cheeks apart, the command came again.

She blinked away a sheen of pink-tinged tears as the small pain from her breasts flowered into a fiery heat between her thighs.

And she watched.

Chanda's strap-on cock bobbed energetically as she neared Mayara. "Do you want to come, slut?"

Chanda's words produced a visible shiver across Mayara's skin. "Oh great ray of light, yessss…" Mayara's teeth were lengthened, resting across her swollen lips and shining slightly as her mouth watered in anticipation.

"Then come you shall. It is my wish that you come."

"I am obedient to your wishes in all things." Mayara shuddered again, her thighs wide and glistening. "I am ready to come, Chanda. Give me the ultimate pleasure. Give it now."

Suliana noticed Chanda's eyes glitter as she approached Mayara.

This one is not to be trusted.

The thought blazed through her mind, and for a moment she could not tell if it was hers or emanated from the man behind her. It was so strong…so absolute.

Chanda's fangs were dripping as she stroked the buttocks that she had so recently lashed with fervor. "You have done well, slut. You deserve your reward."

Mayara was pink and flushed now, her scent rich and heady in Suliana's nostrils.

"Can you smell her? Can you smell her pussy? Smell her juices?" Sharp nails digging into her nipples made Suliana gasp. "She smells good, but you are sweeter. Sweeter and sharper, like the finest moon wine. You smooth the tongue and bite the palate, Suliana."

He squeezed her breasts again and then released them, leaving her bereft and in pain at the loss. "It's a combination that intrigues me. Seduces me. Makes me want to fuck you into insanity while I drain that vintage from your body."

"You would kill me." Suliana hissed the words awkwardly past her lengthened teeth.

Sexual arousal stimulated the canine growth in their species. With orgasm came the desperate need to feed on the heat of a partner. To sustain themselves and each other during the explosion that was climax.

Without the mutual feeding, their mating would result in death. And even then, the feeding was, of necessity, minimal. There were still fatalities. Still deaths in the throes of release. And their numbers were dwindling.

"Kill you?" He laughed, a rough rumbling vibrating against her spine. "Oh no. Or perhaps…yes." His hands dropped to her thighs and at last touched her pussy, spreading the folds and finding the secrets within. "But it would be a divine ending."

He flicked her clit sharply making her bite back a cry of wonderful agony.

"Divine, Suli. For both of us." He rubbed around the sensitive flesh, slicking her juices across her skin and making her writhe in her restraints.

"But for now, you will watch."

She obeyed. There was no other choice for her.

Spellbound by the erotic savagery in front of her and the heat of the man behind her, Suliana watched.

Mayara was freed from her restraints, only to be reattached to a waist-high bench, and bent over it, head turned sideways facing Suliana.

Her body was taut and trembling under the full light of the twin moons. Her fangs shone brightly. Little drops of liquid oozed from their tips, a precious liquid that would heal the scars they left behind.

Suliana's own teeth were leaking the same thing. As were the Master's—drips of desire on her shoulders burned her like acid, and yet she craved more…more pain, more pleasure, the burst of heat on her tongue as she orgasmed and fed from her partner. That mutually magnificent instant of time when the universe ceased to exist and all that was one person opened, melded, blended with another.

She squirmed as Chanda leaned over Mayara, rubbing the cock attached to her groin over the scarred buttocks. There would be release for Mayara. There would be none for Suliana.

The ropes binding her wrists chafed as she tensed, watching Chanda's tongue make a leisurely voyage over Mayara's back, lapping at the wounds, sipping the taste of passion, and bringing whimpers of pleasure to both women's throats.

Chanda adjusted the device and Suliana almost wept, knowing the hard base of the fake cock would be pressing into Chanda's clit, stimulating her, driving her onwards and upwards as she fucked Mayara.

It was a sensation denied Suliana. And the pain of that denial was an arousing pleasure all its own.

She sobbed, biting back the sound, fearing to show weakness.

"Yes, Suli. Yes. You can show us all how you feel…" The Master's cock nudged hard against the tight ring of muscles between her cheeks. There was moisture there now, and she gasped at the heat she felt. The desire she felt rising inside her for his penetration.

She wiggled—an invitation. *Take me. Thrust into my darkest places. Make me yours.*

They were mere thoughts, scampering across her wildly careening brain, but she might as well have spoken them aloud.

For he knew them. Knew her emotions, the exact level of her arousal, and her need to be claimed. He knew that she was responding wildly to the erotic images playing out before her eyes. Knew that she would do *anything* at this moment to feel what Mayara would feel, to share that blinding ecstasy that the two women were about to experience.

"No, Suliana. Not tonight."

And it would be denied her. *He* would deny her.

Mayara was pleading now, grinding her breasts into the wood beneath them, desperately seeking the release she'd been promised.

Chanda leaned over. "Are you ready, my slut?" She held one wrist to Mayara's mouth as she positioned the cock between Mayara's spread legs.

"Yes, mistress. Oh sweet rays, yes. I need you. I need to be fucked *now*. Please...*please*...my cunt aches..."

Suliana saw Chanda's eyes narrow. Once again she was troubled for a brief moment by irrational thoughts about this woman. *Chanda is dangerous.*

The pressure between Suliana's ass cheeks grew harder as Chanda settled herself into position. Her wrist was at Mayara's lips, her mouth nearing Mayara's back.

She was ready.

So was Suliana. Thighs soaked, she moaned as the imitation cock slicked around Mayara's pussy. *I wish it was me. My cunt aches too. My body aches. I cannot stand the denial.*

"Watch, my sweet blood flower. Watch them take their pleasure. Watch them share the bite." The Master continued his torturous narration, forcing her into a place where there was only screaming urgency, only the unattainable peak. He was keeping her back from the top, forbidding her the final leap.

Suliana threw her head back in a spasm of frustrated desire, her skull meeting solid flesh with an unforgiving thud. She could go no further...he held her motionless, his cock pressing against her anus but not pushing within, not fulfilling her need. His fingernails raked harshly over her ass, and she could feel the flesh split in the wake of the sharp talons. It was a little pain, but it pushed her even further along the road to desperation.

Chanda was sweating, and Mayara was sobbing. It was time. Both women were flushing deeply, the pink of their skin muted by the moonlight, but unmistakable even through the mist which was deepening by the minute.

"I claim *Arraho—*" The ancient words of the dominant partner were torn from Chanda's lips.

"I surrender *Arraho—*" screamed Mayara.

Chanda moved slightly and thrust the cock deep into Mayara's ass.

Her cry of agony split the night and sent a chill into Suliana's soul. They were both feeding now, Chanda's mouth buried against Mayara's spine, and Mayara's lips fastened to Chanda's wrist.

But the pain of the unexpected penetration had distracted Mayara, and it was clear that she could not drink sufficiently to overcome it.

Chanda guzzled greedily, her hips pounding against Mayara's ass, slapping them harshly as her teeth drove again and again into the fragile flesh beneath her. Flesh from which the fire of release was fading rapidly.

Chanda ignored it. She continued to pound into the shattered body, and feed from the weakening flow.

"*Enough.*" It was a bark of command from behind Suliana, but she knew it had come too late. Nothing would stop Chanda now.

"*Aaaiiiyyeee…*" The triumphant bellow of orgasm erupted from Chanda's throat as she broke, shuddering from head to foot and pulling her teeth sickeningly from Mayara's flesh. Her breasts shook, her body writhed with pleasure, and droplets of blood splattered onto Mayara's skin, spraying from the elongated fangs that had savaged and fed so thoroughly.

Suliana's arousal died in that instant.

So did Mayara.

In a far-off world, an alternate place to that of Suliana and the Master, a woman woke from a dream. She was soaked with sweat, her thighs slick and aching, her nipples hard to the point of pain, and a scream dragging at her throat.

She turned on the bedside light with a trembling hand.

It was there. The black flower.

Once again the strange black flower with its sickeningly sweet scent had appeared as if by magic next to her bed.

And Sally Ann Moss turned her face into the pillow and wept.

Chapter Two

"So how's my favorite writer today?"

"Julie, I'm your *only* writer." Sally fiddled with the pencil lying next to her notes on the desk.

"So? Doesn't mean you're not my favorite, too."

"Okay. Enough with the editor sucking-up thing. You want to know about the status of the edits, right?"

Julie's attractive chuckle sounded in Sally's ear. "Can't put one over on you, can I? All right. How're the edits coming? We want to go to press with this in time for Halloween. Another S.A. Moss vampire release. Huge sales. Crowds go wild. People line up outside bookstores for hours beforehand."

Sally giggled. "You're laying it on a bit thick you know."

"Sue me. Or better yet, finish those edits so we can both make pots of money and I can afford the lawsuit."

"Wise ass." Sally shook her head. "The edits are almost done. Two chapters left. I'll send it off tomorrow…probably."

There was silence on the other end of the line. "You okay, Sal? You sound — I don't know — tired, maybe?"

"*Me*?" Sally grimaced. "Why should I be tired? I'm churning out more books than humanly possible to feed your need for litigious solvency, living in a world peopled with erotic vampires, pulling plotlines out of my ass with unfailing regularity and you ask if I'm *tired*?"

"Point taken. And thanks for the influx of cash. But seriously — what is it, honey?"

Sally sighed, touched by the concern in her friend's voice. "Didn't sleep well last night. That's all. Honest."

"You need a vacation maybe." There was a slapping sound. "No. I take that back. I just slapped myself upside the head. You don't need a vacation, because if you take one you won't be writing and I will have to explain to management why there isn't another best-selling S.A. Moss book on the horizon."

Laughing, Sally reached for her second cigarette of the day, lit it and took an appreciative drag.

"And quit those damn cigs, will ya?"

"Oh sit on it, Jules. It's my only vice. Without it I'd be perfect, and a god-awful bore."

"So go get a boy toy. Turn lesbian. Find a vice that won't frickin' *kill* you."

"I'm cutting back. Honest. It's just that sometimes, especially after a rough night, they soothe me."

"That bad?" Julie's voice was concerned.

"Yeah. This was a bad one." *Arousing – screamingly erotically arousing – but bad.*

"You need a pill or something? Maybe go get a checkup?"

"Nope." Sally wrinkled her nose. "I'm fine in the mornings. Sometimes I can't even remember what the dream was about. I vaguely sort of remember waking up from it, since of course I don't actually wake up, because the flower's there…"

"A flower?" Julie waited.

"Stupid stuff. Natural, I guess when you consider where my head is for ninety percent of my day."

"I suppose." Julie sighed. "It's got to have some effect on the psyche. Writing darkly savage erotic vampire romances isn't something one can prepare oneself for, is it?"

"You're starting to sound like the PR department blurb, babe."

"'Hey, don't blame me. You write 'em." Julie chuckled. "And they are all of the above, if not more. Readers can't get enough of your purple world and your lusty vampires."

Sally's vision blurred as an image of twin moons in a dark magenta sky swam across her mind. She blinked away the vague echo of a scream.

Like I said. Stupid stuff. Dream stuff.

"Yes." Sally swallowed, struggling to keep her thoughts on track.

"So d'you think this new dream might find its way into another *Scars of the Lash* novel?"

"Possibly." She stared at her monitor, where five thousand words of the story had already unfolded over three cups of coffee. "Probably. I'll let you know."

"Good girl. And I'll wait for those edits, okay? You need extra time, don't sweat it. Readers will buy whatever you write, greedy little revenue units that they are. Perhaps if we keep them waiting a bit, it'll sharpen their appetites."

"Okay. Thanks." Sally stubbed out her cigarette. *I'm gonna quit. I swear. Tomorrow.*

"Talk to you soon."

She was gone before Sally could say goodbye. But that was Julie. Supportive, driven, she was the force behind the success that was S.A. Moss. Without her, it was very unlikely that Sally's wild stories would ever have seen the light of day.

It had only taken one meeting at a romance industry convention, and Julie had latched on to her, firmly believing that Sally had talent, incredible stories to tell and simply needed to get them into the right place.

Which was, of course, with Julie.

It was a mutually beneficial relationship that had deepened into friendship over the past several years, especially as S.A. Moss had become, to Sally's eternal astonishment, a "name" writer. Someone whose books were released in hardcover, to be gobbled up by readers hungry for vampires and sex.

She straightened her shoulders and shoved her unease aside. Time to put the dreams away, forget about them, and get those fucking horrid edits finished. A couple of clicks saved her new work into an untitled folder, and a couple more closed it up. Tight.

Pity her mind wasn't as efficiently organized as her desktop.

She lit another cigarette guiltily and opened the file containing her edits. For now, there was work to be done.

* * * * *

Three weeks later, Sally stretched and arched her aching spine.

There had been no more dreams. No more mysterious flowers, no overwhelming fragrance haunting her nostrils.

Instead, there was three-quarters of a novel on her hard drive. *Scars of the Lash - The Women* was shaping up to be a humdinger of a sex story. Lesbian vampires weren't new, of course, in fact Sally was pretty sure there'd been an article about them in a recent men's magazine.

She chuckled as she saved her work. This one was gonna cross the gender boundaries for sure. What the hell was it with guys and lesbians? Toss a few sharp canine teeth into the mix and readers turned into slobbering, hungering mad people, devouring all the gritty details like a vampire devouring…blood…

…licking…lapping…

A startling vision of a woman bent over another woman shook Sally rigid.

Sheesh. Time to lay off the coffee.

She stretched again, grimacing at the cracks coming from her bones. Twelve hours straight, barring a trip or five to the bathroom, was pushing her physical tolerance to the limits.

But this story burned in her head. It was damn near writing itself.

With a little help from those fucking dreams.

She pushed the thought aside. Time for a wee bit of self-indulgence. Wine, maybe some cheese — there had to be some in the fridge somewhere. Sally vaguely remembered making a sandwich at some point earlier in the day, but hunger, along with most of her other physical needs, took second place when she was in the throes of a novel.

It had always been that way.

Her hand trembled a little as she poured herself a glass of Chardonnay. When had it started?

She must have been about six or perhaps seven years old. A dream that had brought her upright in her pink and frilly bed, screaming loudly, surrounded by stuffed animals who had stared blankly at her.

Her mother had come running, her father close behind, and together they'd calmed a scared child's fears and soothed her, reminding her that dreams weren't real, although they seemed so at the time.

It had helped. A lot. As had the rather frightening drawing she'd produced with her crayons the next day in school. But it had passed, along with so many childhood fears. She'd forgotten about the whole bizarre business until her late teens, when they began again.

A freshman in college by this point, the option of waking up screaming and getting parental cuddles was no longer viable. Sally had learned to bite back the cries, stifle the fear and quell the accompanying arousal.

Sometimes by the touch of her own hand, sometimes by turning to whoever she was in bed with at the time. Several boyfriends had blinked at the ferocity of the lovemaking she'd initiated during the dark hours of the night.

Although, come to think of it, not one had complained.

It was at this time that she'd started writing. Fueled by the visions from her dreams, Sally had penned her first story, a short violent tale of vampires and their conquests. It had taken first prize in the fantasy contest held by a local Goth fraternity, and she'd been hailed as a "visionary", a "voice counter to all pre-defined establishment rules", and offered an honorary pledge, even though she was a woman. One guy paid her the ultimate compliment by referring to her work as "ace jerk-off stuff".

It had only gotten her a B in her lit class, though, since she'd been ignorant of things like point of view and her punctuation sent shudders of horror across her professor's august features.

But the bug had bitten her, if that could be the right way to describe it, and—all punning aside—she'd devoted her spare time to her novels. The chance to attend a romance industry convention and meet other authors was too good to pass up.

One thing had led to another, and Sally had left college with a degree and a signed contract, almost within hours of each other.

The wine soothed her brain, and after a few bites of cheese and crackers, the weariness set in. Time to up the self-indulgence factor. She picked up her wine and headed for her bathroom.

* * * * *

"Reclusive author S.A. Moss professes herself to be just a normal person, in spite of the material she produces on a regular basis. She does, however, admit to one obsession – her bathroom."

Sally grinned as she passed the plaque on the wall. Julie'd had the quote from a print interview cropped and framed by a small porcelain toilet seat. It still made her smile.

And every word was true. She *was* reclusive and she *was* totally obsessed with her bathroom.

Her condo was nothing out of the ordinary, just furnished the way she wanted it and with a very nice view. Her car attracted no untoward attention in the parking lot of the local supermarket, and her clothing was pretty basic—jeans and T-shirts, or sweaters for the winter.

There were one or two smart black suits in the closet for visits to her publisher, and a few evening gowns for the rare times she was forced to make a public appearance, something really high on the "I-don't-want-to-do-this" scale.

Her one extravagance, however, had been to hire the best bathroom designer she could afford, and create a special place for herself where she could luxuriate in sybaritic style. Tonight, as she did every time she walked into it, she was more than glad she'd made that decision.

Gleaming white surfaces reflected the many soft lights that shone from the high ceiling. It was painted pure blue, dappled with white clouds by the hand of an artist, and at night the lights could be dimmed to an approximation of a twilight sky.

Ferns and fronds, both silk and real, trailed high and low along the walls, adding a dimension to the room and making it almost like a very well plumbed greenhouse rather than a functional toilet with all the trimmings. There was a gardenia plant that had declared itself to be sublimely happy on a ledge in front of one of the large Palladian windows. Occasionally it deigned to fill the room with the magnificent scent of abundant blooms.

The windows themselves were discreetly leaded and screened, but most often Sally left the one that faced the distant hills bare of blinds. Especially when she kept the lights low as she did now.

Her spa-type tub beckoned, and she turned on the faucets, adding a helping handful of relaxing herbal salts.

Within a few minutes she was stretched out and luxuriating in the gentle bubbles produced by the tiny jets under the surface of the water. Her head nestled perfectly into the appropriate inflatable pillow, her favorite music filled the room, the water smelled and felt divine and she sighed with pleasure.

This was worth the hours she slaved over her stories.

S.A. Moss reaped the very personal rewards of writing best-selling books, closed her eyes, and unwound. Her alter ego, Sally Ann, just vegged out.

Chapter Three

While the knots in her body relaxed under the effects of a soothing water massage, the knots in Sally's mind loosened with the wine and the steamy scent of lavender and lilacs.

She lay almost submerged, water lapping at her breasts and bubbling quietly around her hips. The music swam on the steam, rising to the ceiling and then back to Sally, adding to the deliciously decadent bathing experience.

It was joy through plumbing. Meditation without the crossed legs and navel thing.

It was also the perfect prescription for the end of a long, hard day's writing.

Funny thing about this story. There was no well-defined alpha hero, pouncing on necks and thrusting himself into virgins, willing and otherwise. Sure, basically the plot revolved around the lesbian vampire village, but somewhere there should've been a guy for readers to hang their hat on. A guy who could perhaps redeem one of the less enthusiastic women, turn her straight and then munch on her while he fucked her until her eyeballs rolled.

Or something like that.

Sally closed her eyes and tried to envision such a hero. His voice would be low, quiet but commanding, deep in tone and with an edge to it as he whispered words meant to lure the unwary…to seduce…

Watch, Suliana.

She jerked, slid and spat out a mouthful of bathwater. Where the hell had *that* come from?

The dream. Sally shivered in spite of the warmth. That damned dream. His voice. She had heard his voice—but not seen him. *Him. The Master.*

Something somewhere had opened a window in her mind. The lesbian vampires…the beating, the savage sex…it came back to her, much more clearly than any dream ever had in the past.

Usually they were vague memories by morning, a flicker of an image here and there, something about a flower—a black flower—and a purple sky with two moons. They were inconsistent, but sufficient to plant ideas in her brain that metamorphosed into her stories, plots set in an outlandish world peopled with oversexed vampires.

Her nipples hardened as she remembered the dream in greater detail than she had thought possible.

These weren't undead vampires. They were very much alive. Breathing, fucking, punishing—bleeding dark blood. And overseeing it all was *him*. The faceless Master who had stood so close behind her and thrust his cock between her butt cheeks.

Oh God, how she'd wanted him. And up the ass, too, of all places.

Sally hadn't tried anal very often, but she confessed to herself that in her dream she'd have welcomed it.

Without conscious thought, her thighs parted, the memory of his voice and his words enough to start her pulse throbbing and her pussy aching. She swallowed, realizing that a pulse of water was shooting up her thigh and caressing her clit.

It felt—wonderful.

She let her hands glide downwards, tracing the route from her breasts to her thighs that the Master had taken in reverse. There were no trails of blood following her passage this time, no sting of wounded flesh. Just the touch of her own fingertips.

She pressed against the base of her stomach. So soft, so warm. The blood pulsed beneath her palms. She could almost hear it.

Shit. What the hell was the matter with her? Were her characters creeping into her subconscious? Was that what this was all about? She had no man in her life, no hot sex going on between the sheets? So she was creating an environment for herself where she could indulge her darkest fantasies?

Hmm. Maybe therapy was in order.

Sally blushed. *Riiiiiight.* She was going to lie on a couch and tell some bearded academic all about her erotically decadent dreams.

That was so *not* going to happen.

But *this* was.

Closing her eyes, Sally surrendered to her urges. Her thighs were spread wide, her pussy hot with need. Slipping a hand between her legs, she touched herself, learning her own skin, her own folds of slick flesh, jets of water adding their own caresses to the stimulation.

She found her clit hard and emerging from its hiding place. Too sensitive to bear the sensation of her fingers, she played around and beside it, stroking fast, then slow, then faster again as her buttocks tightened with pleasure.

She backed off, remembering from one of her own books that an orgasm delayed is pleasure tripled. And it was true. Again and again she brought herself to the edge, then withdrew, finding her nipples with her fingers and pinching them, pulling them, teasing herself to a plateau of arousal.

Her hands become other hands. Her touch that of a lover, someone who knew her intimately and could arouse her more than anyone else in the universe. She allowed herself the pleasure of sensing her own skin, its texture at the curve of her hips, its softness beneath her breasts.

The small irregularities at the edges of her nipples, and their hard center, alive with nerve endings that sent bolts of shattering arousal directly to her gut. All features of her own body, all vibrating beneath her own touch. And all, somehow, new to her at this moment.

It was oddly as if she was making love to another, and yet experiencing it herself. Her breasts were hot and swollen, flushing as the blood rushed to expanded vessels beneath the skin. Carrying the merest brush of a fingernail, amplifying it, turning it into the most erotic caress.

She pinched her nipples again—harder this time, something deep inside aching for the pain that would accompany her action. She ached, but not from any self-inflicted agony. She ached to be pushed past this experience into a deeper level, one where she could explode in a dark upheaval, an eruption of her soul.

Her fingers curved into talons, and she clawed at her neck, her shoulders, feeling an answering response deep in her cunt. Her pussy throbbed now, screaming and weeping hot juices into the pulsating water.

She lifted her breasts high, gasping as the cool air hit the hot flesh. She pulled them, squeezing them together cruelly, desperate for something…some sensation that was missing.

Whatever it was, Sally couldn't find it. And at this point, she didn't care. She let herself be overwhelmed by the need to come.

She released her nipples and let her hands slide downwards once more to her clit, the center of her private erotic universe. The water sloshed around her as her neck arched— taut with desire, aching for release.

This time…*this* time she would not hold back.

The surrounding liquid cradled Sally as she rubbed the delicate folds of flesh, faster now, responding to the pulse that pounded from her heels to her ears. Eyes closed, she followed where her body led, moving this way and that, sensing a pattern emerging, a need that could not be denied.

Her folds burned, and she parted them, thrusting two fingers deeply into her cunt. Slick hot juices covered her fingers as they strummed an ancient rhythm, and she opened her mouth on a silent scream.

This time...yes...*this* time...

Sally let go. She opened herself to the orgasm, knowing from the tingles at the base of her spine that she could not stop now. It was the inevitable slide that would take her to the depths of climax, the heights of sensation and a vortex that would swallow her whole.

Now...yes...*now*.

She screamed. "*Arraho...I surrender.*"

The cry came unbidden on a wave of sensation the likes of which threatened to blow her head off.

She trembled and shook as spasms rocked her, her ass clenched uncontrollably and her legs shuddered with the force of it. Great clamping shivers wrenched her cunt, sending currents and eddies into the tub between her legs.

It was blinding, shattering and exhausting.

"*Holy fucking shit.*" Sally panted as the wrenching experience faded, leaving her limp in the bathwater. Why had that been so...intense? And what the hell was that word she'd yelled at her peak?

A dull headache gnawed at the base of her skull.

Enough with the wine. Enough with the sex. I need sleep.

And sleep she got.

But not restful sleep. Not restorative sleep that would refresh her and allow her to wake the next morning energized and ready for work.

Oh no.

On *this* night, the dream came again.

* * * * *

"*Ahh, Suli. You cannot find what you need by yourself.*"

He was pitying her, playing with her, she knew. Breathing against her shoulders, smoothing her skin, stroking her back much as one would pet an animal.

31

Her arms were chained this time, outstretched on either side of her body, secured to God-knew-what. Her ankles, however, were free. She could move her legs, alter her position, shift her weight—at least she had that much going for her.

And once again she was nude.

It seemed unremarkable, since everybody else was, too. More people filled the little glade than before. Couples, singles, there seemed to be a small crowd gathered to...to what?

Suliana didn't know.

But she sensed something, an anticipation perhaps, that sent a prickle of arousal up her spine to meet the unease that lurked in her mind.

There was music of a sort—soft melodious harmonies that sounded strange yet exciting. She could not place the tunes or the instruments, but they were familiar, as were the moves of the dancers swaying in time with the rhythms.

Men clasped each other in tight embraces, women stroked their own skin, breasts were suckled and cocks lengthened as the music increased in tempo. It was decadent, thrilling and made Suliana strain at her chains to join them.

To be stroked and suckled and let the madness overwhelm her.

"Watch, Suliana. There is much you have yet to see." He was still there. Always there. Behind her where she could not catch a glimpse of him other than his strong hands as they fondled her.

The Master.

Three bodies separated themselves from the dance and neared Suliana. Two men, striking in appearance, and one woman, eyes downcast.

"May we, Master?" One man looked past Suliana.

"You may." Permission was granted on a breath that slithered over Suliana's shoulder and down to her nipples. They hardened painfully in response to the mere brush of air.

"Leet?" The man turned back. "Yes, Master?"

"Use Talot. Let Vinnia play too."

A grin spread across Leet's face as he nodded. "Indeed. She shall play."

Suliana stood quietly, fearing to move lest she touch that heated body behind her.

"You would like to play too, wouldn't you, Suli?" A tongue dipped into the hollow of her neck. "I can smell you. Taste the need as it oozes from your skin." His fangs pierced her flesh—a pinprick, no more—but sufficient to produce a drop of her blood.

"Mmm. Good." His lips fastened on the tiny wound and sucked.

Suliana felt the ripple of sensation like a lightning bolt sizzling through her body to her cunt. She moaned.

"Just a taste. A sip. Perhaps next time I shall taste you *here*." He slid his hands to her breasts and found her nipples, pinching them tightly between thumb and forefinger. "You'd like that, wouldn't you? A quick sharp pain, then the wonder of my mouth drinking from you. Making your body weep for me. Making you wet. Ready for fucking."

Suliana swallowed. Her fangs were growing rapidly, pressing hard against a lower lip that was swelling with blood, with need, with desire.

Yes. She would like that. She would like that a *lot*.

"And then I shall drink from *here*…" One hand slid down to her pussy, forcing its way between her thighs.

Without volition, she widened her stance, giving him access to her moist secrets. She was wet already, aroused and waiting for whatever pleasures he would give her. Or withhold from her. Either way, she was ready.

His fingers delved deep, roughly parting her pussy lips, pulling at her clit and bringing tears to her eyes. She squirmed.

He held her still. "This is *mine*, Suli. Mine to rip from your body with my fangs if I so choose." His touch gentled to a stroke that made her sob with pleasure. "Or to caress until you beg me to fuck you. Until you beg me to bury myself inside you and pound your womb. Until your fangs scream out to be locked within my flesh just as my fangs will be locked in yours."

Suliana whimpered, her hips thrusting forward, her mouth opened on a silent cry.

"It will be incredible, Suli. Beyond our imagination." He trailed her moisture up over her mound to her navel, where he ringed the sensitive indentation. "But it won't be yet."

Tears dropped from her cheeks onto her breasts, but she spoke not a word. It was as if his power was holding her voice hostage.

"I know you ache. I know your needs. I am the only one who can fulfill them, Suliana."

He leaned into her, his cock hard between them, the planes of his chest forcing her body forward against the chains securing her. "And it will hurt. It will be magnificent agony."

He pulled at her hips, smacking them back into his groin. His cock forced her cheeks apart, but as before, he would not push forward. He would not penetrate her, nor would he release her.

"I am seduced by the taste of you. I cannot resist. Let me give you a glimpse." She felt the softness of his hair brush her cheek, then the sharp piercing of his fangs as he ripped into her neck.

The blood ran over her chest to her breasts, a burning flood that heightened the whirl of passion enveloping her.

Suliana screamed, for once giving voice to her pleasure. Hips thrusting wildly, her legs trembled with the urge to lock around someone — *anyone* — and pull a cock into her heat. To ease the pleasure-pain of the orgasmic shudders that shook her to her soul by fucking her, taking her, claiming her. Sending her off the edge of the vast chasm that now yawned before her, revealed by the bite of the Master.

He released her, sighing as his fangs slid from her flesh, licking the healing juices across the gaping wound. It tingled, sealing rapidly.

"*Suliana*. Great ray of light, *Suliana*. It will be...*incredible*." His fingers tightened on her hips. "But for now, you must watch. Only watch."

And she gulped down a sob as she heard the tremor in his voice.

Chapter Four

Obedient to the Master's command, Suliana watched the scene unfolding before her.

Leet and Vinnia secured Talot's wrists to a bar high above his head. His body flexed as the strain showed in his muscles, but his cock remained hard, protruding eagerly from his body as the others circled him, slapping him occasionally with open hands.

Vinnia pulled a small whip from a jeweled box at the edge of the glade. It had many short lashes, rather than one, and they seemed to be made of something softer than the usual single braids.

It still worked, though.

Suliana's eyes opened wide as Vinnia brought it up swiftly beneath Talot's cock, catching his balls at the same time.

His cry was one of pain but the look on his face spoke of nothing but pleasure.

Leet circled him, standing behind him, and rubbing himself against Talot's back. "Shall I fuck you, darling?" Leet's teeth had lengthened, as had Talot's and Vinnia's. They were excited, their sexual arousal glowing from every pore.

"If it is your pleasure." Talot's eyes swiveled from Vinnia and the flogger to Leet, hiding just out of view.

"You have such a wonderful ass. So hard in all the right places and so soft in others." Leet looked down, his actions hidden from Suliana by Talot's body.

Vinnia reached for Talot's cock and stroked it, her touch becoming a grasp and her grasp becoming a death grip, as Leet continued to do whatever it was he was doing behind Talot.

Struggling against his bindings and writhing with eagerness, Talot shouted. Vinnia dropped his swollen cock, reached for her whip and lashed it hard, the tails of the flogger whistling through the air as she struck again and again.

Talot's hips thrust forward into the attack, propelled from behind by Leet.

Suliana's eyes widened as she realized Leet was fucking Talot in the ass, savagely pounding their bodies together in concert with Vinnia's whipping.

Vinnia moaned as Talot's cock leaked traces of pink-tinged semen, droplets of pre-come that glistened against the dark purple head.

It was a sound that distracted both men and their heads turned toward her.

"I...I...*need*—" She stared at them, reaching for Talot's cock once more, her thighs dewed with the silken drool from her cunt. Her nipples budded hard atop small high breasts, and her fangs dripped as she licked the moisture from their tips.

She repositioned the flogger and lashed it between her own legs. "Oh...oh..."

Suliana could see Vinnia's buttocks clenching as each blow fell on her pussy. She was in ecstasy, driving her own orgasm, reaching higher as the lashes fell harder on her flesh.

"Leet. Take her. Take *Arraho*." The Master's chest rose and fell against Suliana's spine as he gave the abrupt command.

Leet tore himself from Talot's body, his cock enormous and shining from the penetration. He grabbed Vinnia, thrusting her against Talot, who still hung by his arms, fangs dripping, panting with lust.

Wedged between the two men, Vinnia shrieked with eager anticipation, parting her thighs and offering her cunt to Leet.

Muscles bunched as Leet raised her, letting her wrap her legs around him and positioning her for his pleasure.

Without a word, Leet thrust into her, using such force that Suliana could hear their bodies slap together. He continued to thrust, forcing the air from Vinnia's lungs in harsh screaming gasps and making Talot struggle against his bonds and the abrasion of Vinnia's back.

Vinnia's eyes rolled back in her head, her teeth protruded past her lips and she lashed her head forward into Leet, biting into the hardness of his chest and securing herself to him.

Leet howled and bit Vinnia in turn, finding her shoulder and ripping at it with a desperate hunger. They fed and orgasmed, one activity indistinct from the other. Bodies trembled, throats gasped and swallowed and hips thrust frantically, prolonging the experience and driving Suliana nearly mad with lust as she watched.

"We shall do better." Another nip to her earlobe pierced the fragile skin, and it was all Suliana could do not to surrender to her own *Arraho*. She knew in her heart what that word meant. *Orgasm.* And so much more.

But with consummate skill, the Master held her back, giving only enough to keep her sexually aroused, wet with her juices and shuddering, but never more than that. Never allowing her the release he had driven her body to crave.

It was almost like dying with each breath.

But Suliana would not surrender. It was not in her nature. She fought against her body's needs. Struggled with the desires that ravaged her. And refused to surrender. When the time came, she would choose to *share* her *Arraho*.

"Yes. You are strong, my Suli. Very strong." Hands stroked the length of her arms to her wrists and caressed their way back to her body, cupping her breasts. "Let's see how strong you are."

Oh great ray of light. What now?

* * * * *

"Talot."

The man's head jerked up, looking away from Vinnia and Leet who were collapsed at his feet and toward Suliana.

"Free yourself."

The Master's command was instantly obeyed. With a twist and a tug, Talot was free.

"Come here. To Suliana. Take your own *Tapaha*."

Tapaha. An orgasm of lesser intensity. No feeding, just pleasure. The word rang in Suliana's ears.

"And don't hold back." The Master's hands squeezed her breasts tightly, making her gasp. "She will know. So will I."

He flicked her nipples cruelly, and Talot's fangs lengthened in response. He nodded, eyes fixed on the mounds swelling within the Master's hands.

"Thank you." Talot's response was surprisingly mild. And yet his gaze burned hot as his hand reached down for his cock, gripping it hard and stroking it from base to tip.

Suliana watched, fascinated and aroused, as Talot caressed himself. His fingers wrapped firmly around his cock and he slowly began his own ascent, sometimes tugging on the skin, at others letting his hand slide loosely along the shaft.

"Spread your legs, my Suli." The Master nudged her ass with his knee, enforcing his command.

She obeyed, still watching Talot as he masturbated in front of her.

The Master's touch made her jump as he slipped a hand between her thighs, smearing her juices over her skin and his fingers. "Talot…"

Talot stepped nearer, close enough for the Master to reach him.

Suliana choked as one strong hand, glistening with her own hot silken moisture, joined the Talot's hand, and in concert they moved.

She was so close between them now, close enough that Talot could have fucked her if he moved forward just an inch or so more. She wanted him to.

She wanted that hard cock inside her cunt. She wanted his body pounding into hers and she wanted his sharp fangs to rip her flesh, suckle her blood and send her spinning into the well of ecstasy.

A rough chuckle sounded in her ear. "He is beautiful, isn't he? Something to be savored. Tasted. Fucked."

The Master was moving behind her, his cock hard, rubbing against her ass. He'd released Talot, and returned to holding *her*, preventing her from pushing her cunt onto Talot's hard and shining length.

Suliana felt, more than saw, the presence of others around them. Sighs and moans began to fill the glade, lit now by only one moon. Shadowy shapes materialized around the little group, as more and more bodies began the slow ride to *Tapaha*.

Talot's mouth opened wide and he hissed past his fangs, eyes lowered to his hand as it moved faster now, jerking the skin hard then releasing it. A bead of moisture appeared at the swollen tip, oozing from the slit.

Drips of liquid fell from his teeth, mixing with his pre-come and slicking his hands.

He panted, as did those around him. Women neared him, touching themselves, staring at his cock as they plunged their fingers deep into their bodies.

A few men stood close too, imitating Talot's movements, their fangs gleaming and twinkling like hard starlight.

It was as if this entire strange world held its breath, trembling on the brink of release.

Suliana held her own breath, heated as much by the friction of the Master's cock as by the sight of Talot in front of her.

The women began to surrender. "*Tapaha.*" The mewling cry was echoed by others as, one by one, they succumbed to the pleasure of their own touch, shuddering on their feet or falling to the ground and writhing through the delight.

The sound increased as louder voices cried out, the men spewing seed into the night air, the women convulsing in the throes of their release.

Talot was nearly there.

Suliana raised her eyes to look at him. His pupils were dilated, his irises glowing with the fire of a brilliant amethyst. And behind her, the Master was breathing hard, sliding his cock through his own moisture and between her ass cheeks.

Finally, Talot surrendered too. "*Tapaha.*" He grunted the word, spitting it out from his gut and groaning as his cock jerked, pulsed and erupted jets of hot come onto Suliana's belly and thighs.

Behind her, the Master let go as well. "*Tapaha*, my Suli. *Tapaha.*"

Her back burned as his seed flowed across her skin, pouring down her spine to cross her buttocks in a stream of savage heat.

She was soaked in semen, mixed with the tears of desire pouring from her cunt. Suliana sobbed out loud, desperate to take her own *Tapaha.*

It was not *fair.* It was painful, an ache that could not be eased. A need unmet, a desire unfulfilled.

The scent of orgasm flooded the glade, and the women neared Suliana, fangs bared and wet.

She blinked.

They knelt around her, their faces blurred by the tears that filled Suliana's eyes.

"Yes, children. Taste her. Taste she who will be mine."

The Master pulled away from Suliana's body, to be replaced by the women who were eyeing her hungrily. One ventured closer, licking the seed from her skin. Another followed. Soon she was surrounded, being touched by many tongues, many hands.

One went further, nipping her flesh and drawing blood.

That was all it took.

Suliana screamed as what felt like a thousand mouths began to devour her, to suckle the mixture of semen and blood that now dappled her belly, her buttocks and her thighs.

There was pain, and there was incredible delight as the tongues and the fangs connected with her sexual organs, sending her cunt into spasms of need and her clit into granite-like rigidity.

She wept, from her eyes and her pussy, the pink moisture trickling down to blend with the other liquids on her body. Each suckling touch, each piercing bite—and Suliana rose one notch higher on her personal arousal scale.

Her vision began to swim as her breaths grew choppy and harsh—she could not take much more without *Tapaha*, *Arraho* or oblivion.

A hand reached around to the front of her leg and slashed a wound from knee to hipbone. Screams of pleasure followed as tongues fought to find the best and freshest blood.

The other leg was slashed, a blinding pain that she felt in her nipples, her belly and deep inside her womb.

It was too much. She would not surrender. She opened her mouth and cried out the only word that would pass the constriction in her throat.

"*Kyreeeeehaaa!*"

* * * * *

Her own scream woke her.

Sally jerked upright, shuddering in pain and desperate to touch her pussy, to relieve the ache of unfulfilled orgasm.

Kyreeha. It rang in her ears. *What does it mean?*

I challenge.

The answer flooded her mind clearly, as clearly as the agony she felt in her gut and her legs. With trembling hands she pushed aside the covers.

There were scars crisscrossing her belly, and two long welts traversing her thighs.

She gasped, and sucked in a sweet scent. One she knew in her subconscious mind, one she recognized.

Slowly, almost terrified to look, Sally turned her head toward the bedside table.

It was there.

The black flower, delicate and shimmering, each petal dark yet luminescent, it sat on the polished wood. The fragrance was unique, unmistakable, swimming through the bedroom to fill Sally's nostrils and her mind.

She looked again at her body. The red scars were beginning to fade, to diminish before her eyes. The pain dulled, softened and vanished.

She swallowed and glanced once more at her bedside table.

The flower had disappeared.

Sally's mind gave up the struggle to understand. There was no reason, no comprehension for any of this.

Her brain shut down, her body collapsed and she fainted.

Chapter Five

The Master's boots clicked sharply as he walked to the center of the quiet room. There were few lights here, only enough to illuminate the woman lying on the cold marble slab.

No windows, no openings, just a stone walled crypt containing the future of his race. Shadows brushed her face, highlighting the cheekbones and the silvery white hair that fell to her shoulders. He knew her eyes would be lavender if—*when*—they were open.

But now they were closed, her features expressionless, her body still as the dead. It was hard to believe that her spirit had taken form and shared the Glade with him, and yet it had. Mistresses always did, beginning the process of their return by materializing for short periods of time and then leaving, softly shimmering away to nothing until the next time in the Glade— and the next—

"Ahh, Suli. When will you awaken? When will you come and take your rightful place beside me? Why do you wait?"

Noul Keirat, Master of his world, laid warm hands on the cold ones crossed so peacefully beneath Suliana's breasts. He dipped his head and dropped a kiss on each pale peak, tired to his soul, and weary of this ritual.

He wanted his mate. He wanted *Arraho*. With her.

Once again, like so many Masters before him, he cursed bitterly, ranting against the fate that had condemned him to suffer this agony. This separation of the Master and his Mistress prior to their linking, their joining.

Keirat cursed the Ancient Ones who had decreed that each ruling couple must be worthy of the rank, strong enough to control their people, and committed to eternity with each other.

The concept of removing a portion of each potential Mistress's soul had been born in the far distant past. It had been done of necessity.

The Raheeni were a violent and warlike people. They had to be, to survive and flourish on their world. Condemned by the harsh conditions on the surface, they spent half the year underground in cities within caverns built eons before by artisans whose names were lost to the passage of time.

The other half of the year was spent above, reaping what harvests they could, and mating. Invasions had been repelled, and strangers from other planets were not welcomed. Too many "visitors" had regarded the purple planet as a useful target for a variety of projects, none of which met with the Raheeni's approval.

There had been wars. Too many wars. Both external and internal. For the savagery that characterized the Raheeni was part of their nature, and essential for their survival.

After one particularly vicious and bloody coup, the Ancient Ones had made their fateful decree. To rule, the Master and Mistress must prove their worth — their strength. And to protect those most suited, there would be a time of "separation". She who possessed the requisites for the Mistress-to-be would be *cleaved*, halved, leaving the shell of the woman on Raheen, and placing her spirit elsewhere for protection.

If she was strong enough to return, to withstand the Glade of Arraho, then she was worthy. The Master would have enough to do to protect himself.

It had worked. For many generations since that time, suitable candidates for the rank of Mistress had been "cleaved", their spirits seeded across the galaxy by some mechanism unknown to the Raheeni. It just happened.

One day they were normal Raheeni women. The next, their hair silvered, and they fell where they stood, lapsing into a cold, catatonic state. They were ceremonially transported to these crypts, to await the Master's coming.

Each Master would claw his way to the top and then select his mate. For Keirat, there had been no question. He was intelligent, strong, had defeated more challenges than he could remember, and knew — without a single doubt — that Suliana was his.

He had dutifully visited all the crypts, a dozen or so of them, each containing the body of a woman.

But one glimpse at Suli and he *knew*.

What was worse was the knowledge that she shared his response. His reactions, his emotions — they were hers as well.

They'd linked minds and souls over the course of time, each interaction becoming more sensual, more arousing, until by now, Suli should have made the conscious choice to return to her body. To surrender her soul to her Master.

But she had challenged him.

Something was different about this woman. Perhaps that was what had attracted Keirat in the first place. The determination of that firm chin. The spirit of independence and curiosity he sensed within her when they met as Raheeni in the Glade.

The fiery sexuality that boiled inside her and threatened to consume him. He'd taken *Tapaha*, for the ray's sake. Spewed his seed across her ass like any raw youngster.

He rubbed his face with his hands and sighed. He was tired. Being Master was so much more than fucking, although few realized it. There were Elders who quietly ran the business of life for the Raheeni. But his was the ultimate voice. Decisions had to be made, often life and death decisions.

Their survival depended on his strength. He must not lose it now. He must win Suliana, bring her back to her body, seduce her soul.

He had to overcome her resistance, lure her to his side, and rule with her, breeding future generations of leaders with her, raising them in the safety of their underground world.

To do otherwise would be to betray weakness. There were factions who waited for exactly that—weakness on the part of the Master. Power was to be desired, seized if at all possible. Many would try to take his power and position by force, should he falter.

Keirat's world was a savage one. But it was *his*.

And so was Suliana.

He left her body and keyed in the code to unseal the crypt. The lights dimmed to mere flickers behind him as the door slid shut once more.

"She is weak."

Chanda leaned against the passage wall, watching him as he emerged. "She will not survive. I would be a better choice."

Keirat's mouth firmed as he stood still, eyeing this woman he neither trusted nor liked. "The choice is not yours to make."

She moved, nearing him. "No. But it *is* yours." Her hands drifted over his chest, and she licked her lips. "The pleasures we could share, Noul Keirat." She dropped her gaze pointedly to his crotch. "Your cock in my cunt. My hot and wet cunt. Slick and ready for you. My teeth in your neck, suckling you, making you harder than you can imagine. Your hands on my breasts, my hands...mmm. Where should I put my hands?"

Keirat stood motionless as she rubbed her body against his, making it quite clear that her pussy was heated and ready.

"You are not a chosen one, Chanda. You may mate where you please. But not with me."

Her fangs glinted slightly as she hissed at him. "And if I win the challenge, *Master*, I shall take her life. I shall drink her spirit and claim her birthright. And then I shall claim *you*. Are you strong enough to survive it, I wonder? Or will there be a new Master perhaps?" She snickered. "Kael Melet is strong. He would not shirk. His cock is huge. He fucked me well, the other night. Our *Arraho* was stupendous. We fed and fucked and fucked again. *He* might well have what it takes to rule." She sneered at him.

Keirat felt his lips twist in disgust as his own fangs lengthened. "Do not put me to the test. You can die as easily as Mayara." He leaned closer and whispered. "*Count on it.*"

* * * * *

For days after waking from her horrific dream, Sally Ann Moss was a driven woman. She barely ate, ignored her phone, and spent endless hours in front of her computer, desperate to finish *The Women*, and equally desperate to write *The Challenge*.

She'd never had two books on the go at once—it was unheard of, even for her.

But there was some force driving her on, some desperate urge to get these two stories into words before—

Before I go insane.

She'd diverted time away from her work to research obscure mental illnesses, stigmata and anything else she could think of that would explain what she had seen—what she had felt—on her own body.

To try and find an explanation for the unexplainable, to understand the incomprehensible, and to reassure herself that her sanity was intact.

She'd failed at all of them. And even worse was the fact she couldn't get the thought of the Master out of her head. She lusted, yearned and desperately fought against the urge to take a quick nap and see if he was lurking in a dream.

Frequently she unzipped her jeans and touched her body, checking to see if any marks had appeared. They had been there, she knew it. She'd felt them, felt the hunger of the voracious mouths as they fed on her, felt the blood as it leached from her veins and capillaries.

She'd felt *his* fingers as he'd ripped her thighs open and encouraged the others to feed. And she'd *seen* that fucking flower. She knew, without a doubt, she'd seen it.

Scared to sleep since she was afraid she might not wake up, she spent her days *and* nights at her desk, dozing fitfully on crossed arms when her eyelids would no longer stay open. Showers were quick, hurried affairs, and nothing mattered any more except her writing…and the overwhelming fear that her life was shattering.

She denied herself sexual release. To her mind, there might be a link between the orgasm she'd had in the tub and the dream that followed. So…no more orgasms.

Equally unsettling was the subject matter she was including in *The Challenge*. Scene after scene of bondage — BDSM — a theme she'd touched on prior to this novel, but never in such exquisite depth.

Sally had joined groups, talked to people who lived the lifestyle, learned every iota of information she could about the "scene".

And it turned her on. She squirmed on her chair as words flew from her fingertips detailing floggings, spankings, the mixture of pain and pleasure that was said to heighten one's orgasmic response. She ordered books, reading a chapter or two here and there when they arrived and then more when her fingers cramped over her keyboard.

She ordered a flogger, but found it ineffective when used on oneself. That was flagellation, she knew, and best left to monks.

She ordered nipple clamps, wincing at the pinch, but aroused by the sensation of painful pleasure that shuddered through her body, both at their application and even more upon their removal.

She was deeply disturbed, worried that she was sinking into some kind of sexual depravity that would swallow her whole.

And behind it all, there was the memory of the dreams.

No wonder I'm afraid to sleep.

The brief naps she took were untroubled by visions of vampire worlds and sensual eroticism. They usually ended when her neck cramped, and were followed by a period of stretching, wincing and a couple of aspirin.

She lost weight, without even realizing it, doubtless because she forgot to eat when immersed in her writing.

And eventually, after the frenzy had gone on for over a month, it brought Julie to her door.

Chapter Six

"Okay, Mohammed. The mountain is here." Julie struggled with bags and boxes as she pushed her way into the condo past a befuddled Sally.

"Huh?"

"You haven't answered your phone or your email in God knows how long. You've pretty much dropped off the face of the planet. I know you like this *reclusive* thing, but you've gone too far with it this time."

She unloaded everything in the kitchen and turned, hands on hips, to stare at Sally. "What the fuck is going on?"

Sally's mouth gaped. "What do you mean?"

Julie opened a large box and pulled out a piece of pizza. "Sit. Eat. Tell me why the hell you're invisible all of a sudden, why you look like shit and what the devil you mean by scaring the crap out of me."

Sally ran hands through her hair. "I haven't a clue what you're talking about." Her nose twitched. "But I gotta say that pizza smells good."

Julie pulled another piece from the box and waved it at Sally. "When did you eat last? Look at you. Those jeans are baggy." She munched at the food. "Bitch."

An unwilling chuckle crept from Sally's throat. It felt — *good*. "I was working. Hard. For you, as a matter of fact. You know what I'm like when I get into the writing."

She picked off the olives from the pizza slice and stared appreciatively at what was left. "You got an everything-on-it one, didn't you?"

"Yep." Julie licked her lips. "Except anchovies."

"Well thank the good Lord for that." Sally dug in. To her surprise, she realized she was starving. Perhaps Julie's intervention had been a good thing. She needed something—*someone*—to yank her back from the edge of her madness. To remind her that there was a normal world outside her door, where people ate pizza on a regular basis, and disdained anchovies.

"Here." Julie passed her a beer. "Wash it down with this."

"Um…on an empty stomach?"

"Fill the stomach with pizza. Who cares? You're not going anywhere. Get drunk. Unload. Tell me about it."

"About what?" Sally mumbled the words around a mouthful of cheese and pepperoni.

Julie took a long swig of her beer and set the bottle down decisively. "Okay. Here's the thing. Some of your research book orders got sent to you, care of me." She nodded at a bag on the floor. "In there is a book on mental illnesses, dream analysis, a couple of BDSM how-to manuals, and a scholarly treatise on stigmata."

Sally twisted the top off her own beer. "So?"

Julie stared at her. "Sweetie, individually, they're not really important. But put together with each other, a woman who has pretty much vanished into thin air, and what you've said in the past about your dreams, a picture emerges. I worry." She picked up her beer and glared at Sally. "I worry *a lot*."

The concern in Julie's eyes was evident, even though her words were businesslike and rapped out in her usual staccato fashion.

Sally sighed. "I'm sorry. Honest. I didn't mean to scare you." She took another slice of pizza. "And you're right. I'm hungry, out of touch, and lost in my stupid stories."

"Stories? As in more than one story?" Julie jumped on that right away.

"Yeah. More than one story. Two of 'em, burning my brains. The first is *The Women*, which you know about, and the second…"

"The second?"

"*The Challenge. Kyreeha.*"

Somehow, saying the word aloud to a normal person in her kitchen over a pizza and beer reduced it to what it was—an invented, unreal jumble of sounds that meant nothing. Sort of.

Julie got up from her chair and pulled a few paper towels off the hanger, passing one over to Sally and wiping her own mouth with another. "Hoookay. Let me see if I've got this right. You've got no less than *two* stories going, simultaneously, both set in the vampire world?"

"Yep." Sally nodded.

"And how far along are you with each of 'em?"

"First one's almost done. Second one I'm a bit over half-done with."

Julie shook her head. "No wonder you've been researching mental illness. That kind of writing would drive me nuts as well. Shit, that kind of *editing* would drive me nuts. I probably should keep those books myself."

Sally drank her beer. The food tasted good, the bite of the tart beverage tasted even better and as her body absorbed the nourishment, she felt her fears recede.

God, I'm such a fucking asshole. "Truth is, Julie, I had a real bad dream. Bad enough that I wondered if I was losing my mind."

Julie frowned. "Look, you can get help for this stuff, you know. Dreams like that…well, it's about the subconscious, or dealing with the fact that you hated your mother and wanted to sleep with your father or something, isn't it?"

Sally nearly spewed her drink. "Fuck, no. At least I don't *think* so."

"So you're having nightmares. Okay. You're drowning yourself in a viciously sexual world of bloodsucking vampires for damn near twenty-four hours a day. That's a fact." Julie ticked it off on her fingers. "Which could go a long way to explaining the dream stuff."

"Right." Sally nodded.

"So where does the other research come in? The stigmata, for example? That's creepy stuff, Sal. You getting religious on me? Gonna redeem your vamps or something?"

"No, good God no." Sally laughed. "Can't redeem 'em. My readers would never forgive me." She paused, wondering how much to say. "It's just...well, if you must know, after that last dream I woke up with...marks on me."

"Marks?" Julie's jaw dropped. "What kind of marks?"

Sally waved a hand over her lap. "Like scars. Welts." She swallowed. "Teeth marks."

"Jesus H. *Christ*."

"Yeah, I know. Stupid, isn't it?" Sally blinked the vision away. "I'm thinking, of course, that they weren't really there. It was another one of those times when I dreamed that I'd woken up. You know how you do that?" She glanced across the table.

"Er..."

"It's kind of like when you dream that you're awake, about to take a test or something, then you can't find a pencil, or you're in the wrong place. But it seems so real, you truly *think* you're awake." Sally reached for another beer. "That ever happen to you?"

Julie nodded. "Oh yeah. SATs. I must've taken them six times one night. But..." she paused, pursing her lips. "I never woke up with marks on me from the desk I was sitting in front of."

"But I didn't actually wake up, don't you see? I just *dreamed* that I did." Sally was vehement. It was the only explanation she'd permit herself.

"Hmm. Well, putting that aside for a minute, how about the bondage stuff?"

"Ah." Sally blushed. "Yeah. That."

"Right. *That.*" Julie tapped her fingers on the table. "Give it up, girl."

"There's nothing to give up." Sally looked defensively at Julie. "I'm...interested, is all."

"Ahh." Her editor looked knowing. "*Interested*, huh?" She grinned. "You fucking anybody right now?"

Sally coughed. "Right at this moment, no. I'm eating pizza with you."

"Wiseass. You know what I mean. Anybody in your life? I know—" Julie held up her hand. "You like to keep that stuff private. And I understand. But I'm still asking. Just this once. You seeing anybody?"

Julie shook her head. "Nope. Where am I gonna get the time? Not to mention the energy. All that stuff...makeup, dresses, social stuff. Urgh. Not my style."

"I see." Julie stood and stretched, then burped. "'Scuse me."

Sally watched her with affection as she tidied away the now-empty pizza box, put more beers in the fridge and pulled an enormous package of chocolate chip cookies from one of the shopping bags. "Good God, Julie. After *pizza*?"

"Dessert." Julie ripped the plastic open with a fingernail. "I would've brought plain chocolate, but somehow the cookies just called to me."

"Riiiight." Sally stared at them. "I'm decadent, full of sugar and empty calories and I'm singing your song."

"Yep. So you need a date, huh? Need to get laid."

A spurt of laughter erupted from Sally's throat. "I do not."

"Do too." Julie smirked. "You need to get down and dirty with someone. Maybe get tied up and spanked while you're at it."

"Julieeee!"

"Hey, I don't have a problem with that. It could be fun." Julie stared absently at a cookie. "Come to think of it..." She jerked herself back into the conversation from whatever fantasy she'd been indulging herself with. "But that's neither here nor there."

"Damn straight." Sally blinked.

"Well, the reason I came over, other than to make sure you were still with us, was to tell you that you actually *do* have a date."

"*What*?" Sally's mouth dropped.

"Yep. This Friday. Tom Silver."

"Tom Silver? *The* Tom Silver?"

"Yep."

"The Tom Silver of *Silver's Soldiers*?"

"Yep." Julie smirked.

Sally swallowed. "Lemme get this straight." She stared at her beer as the label on the bottle wavered a little bit before her eyes. "Tom Silver, the mega-best-selling author of the *Silver's Soldiers* series, wants to go out on a date with *me*?"

Julie shifted. "Well...kinda. Kinda sorta."

Sally took a determined bite of cookie. "Explain 'kinda sorta'. What did you do?"

Julie looked innocent. Or tried to. "*Me*? Nothing. I did nothing at all. Tom's in town for a lecture and a dinner on Saturday. He arrives early Friday and there wasn't anybody available to spend time with him Friday night." She shrugged. "He's a nice guy. Very low-key about this stuff. So when I suggested he might wanna have a beer or something with another low-key writer, he jumped at the chance."

"I'll bet." Sally knew how persuasive Julie could be once she set her mind to something.

"No really. He's read your stuff. Said he likes it." Julie grinned. "Dunno if that's true or not, but what the hell. It'll get you out of the house, you can spend time talking author stuff with a fellow writer…what more could you ask?"

Sally sighed.

"Before you say no, I should also add that he's a real good looker, too." Julie waggled her eyebrows. "In fact, the word 'hot' comes to mind."

"I know. I've seen his picture on the back of his books. Figured it was airbrushed."

"Nope. He's the real thing."

"Hot, huh?"

"Yep. 'Here's-my-panties-and-the-catch-on-my-bra-is-at-the-back' type of hot."

"Hmmm."

* * * * *

Several hours later, Sally woke up, astounded to find herself on her own couch, covered in a blanket.

Across the room, Julie was sitting in front of her desk, clicking her way through Sally's files.

"Mmmpff." Sally's mouth was dry, but she was rested. A glance at the clock told her she'd slept longer than she'd done in days. Without a single fang, scream, flower or dream.

Thank God.

Julie turned as Sally stretched and groaned. Her eyes were wide. "Sally. My God, *Sally.*"

"What?"

"These stories. They're…they're…"

"Oh Jesus. You hate them, don't you?" With the insecurity that has plagued writers since the first stylus scrawled "Chapter One" on a bit of scrap papyrus, Sally grimaced.

Julie gulped. "They're *incredible.*" She turned back to the screen and closed the file. "They're beyond anything you've ever written before. I'm—*stunned.*"

"Oh." Sally cleared her throat. "That's...that's good, then, yes?"

Julie nodded, still struggling to find words. That, in itself, was compliment enough, but as always she needed to voice her opinions. "They're dark, darker than ever, which is saying something. But they're powerful, too. It's like I was there. Tied to that tree, being lashed by that dude..." She shook her head. "Turned me on, Sally, I don't mind admitting it."

Sally bit her lip. "Really?"

"Yeah." Julie stood and ran her hands through her short spiky hair. "And it's convinced me more than ever that you need to get yourself fucked, babe. But *good*."

"Jules, I..."

"Nope. Don't wanna hear it." Julie crossed the room, grabbed her coat and purse and headed for the door. "Tom'll be at the bar in his hotel. Seven on Friday. I'll email you with more details. Be there. It's casual, so jeans'll be fine." She grinned. "Take notes."

Which, mused Sally as she headed out on Friday night, was how editors thought, most probably. Take notes, put it in a book, make a mint of money. And if fucking is involved, so much the better.

Well, shit. Julie was doomed to disappointment. There was no way in hell S.A. Moss was gonna fuck Tom Silver.

No way in hell.

Chapter Seven

"You know, I'd really *really* like to fuck you."

It was the truest thing Tom Silver had said lately. He'd unenthusiastically agreed to share a beer with vampire writer S.A. Moss, simply because he didn't like the idea of a night alone in his hotel room.

He'd expected an overly made-up, black-haired Goth-type woman, probably with studs, leather, and maybe fishnet someplace. Her novels were sexually arousing, her vamps savage, and he figured she probably snacked on hemoglobin when nobody was watching.

He'd been dead wrong.

The tall, lithe woman who'd glanced around the bar and finally met his gaze had been completely unlike anything he could've imagined. No wonder she kept her photo off the back of her books. Her vampire readers would have been disappointed, most probably. Tom wasn't. *No sirree.*

His cock stood up, saluted, and *Hoorah*'ed.

Sally was fair, tumbling hair reaching her shoulders in uninhibited waves. Her eyes were the oddest shade of blue, almost purple in some light, and her mouth was generous, smiling warmly with lips that were full and gleamed with a dab of something glossy.

She wore jeans, nice snug jeans that hung to her curves, and a sweater that ramped up Tom's arousal level. It was cut low and slithered over wonderfully full breasts, unashamedly showing cleavage and the soft hills and valleys of a luscious woman.

He'd managed to roll up his tongue, shove it back in his mouth, wipe the drool off his chin and wave to her. All within five seconds of meeting her gaze.

She'd waved back and crossed the room unselfconsciously, hips swaying, long strides bringing her to his table without hesitation.

"Hi. I'm Sally Ann Moss." She held out her hand.

Tom looked at it as he stood. "I know." He grinned. "I'm Tom Silver. Pleased to meet you." He took her hand in his, turned it over and kissed the back of it. Where the fuck that had come from, he had no idea, but it had worked.

She'd gasped, laughed, blushed and sat down, and from then on, the evening had been a delight.

They'd swapped war stories, of course. The publishing world was a complex, challenging valley of depravity at times, peopled with egos, conflicts and deadlines. They had acquaintances in common, shared a dislike of public appearances, and both agreed that "promo" was the tool of the Devil.

The number of empty glasses on their table grew, only to be replaced by full ones. They grew less inhibited with each other, Sally teasing Tom about the lack of sex in his novels and Tom responding that she wrote enough for both of them.

He asked about vampires. She countered by asking him about the military. They shared research techniques, both for writing and content. They discovered different writing styles — hers an uncharted flow of story, his a well-plotted and pre-scripted tale.

Tom was enchanted by her wit, her humor and the sexuality that radiated from every pore of this amazing woman. She leaned forward to make a point, heedless of the fact that her sweater revealed a good portion of her breasts and the merest hint of black lace.

She was getting to him, and what got to him the most was that she didn't seem to realize it. In his entire life he didn't think he'd ever met anyone so unaware of her own appeal.

As the evening wound down, the delightful buzz between them increased. He touched her hand to make a point...she brushed his hair back behind his ear.

They laughed together, smiled at nothing in particular, and when they finally stood, Tom figured she'd catch on to his state of mind, since his cock was harder than iron and his pants did little to hide it.

His words were slightly slurred, but his thoughts crystal clear. "I really, *really* would like to fuck you."

She stepped closer to him, eyes shadowed by her hair. There was a moment of silence as they studied each other. Then Sally reached out and cupped his cheek with her hand. "I think I'd like that, too."

She leaned in and kissed him, a light brushing of lips. "Just one night. One time when we can enjoy ourselves and each other. Writer to writer, man to woman."

"Mmm." Tom's lips sought to keep hers close, but she had pulled away.

"Your room." She had his wrist grasped in hers. "Come on."

He grinned, nodding at the waitress as they left. "You in a hurry?"

She tapped her foot outside the elevator. "Yes." It arrived, and she dragged him inside. As soon as the doors slid shut, she was on him, sliding her body against his, kissing him and driving her tongue into his mouth.

Her hips thrust hard against his and he gasped, covering her lips with his and kissing her back in his turn.

They almost missed his floor.

Tom fumbled his keycard, but finally got the stupid light to turn green. His hands were shaking, his head swimming and his cock throbbing as Sally slid her hand down the front of his pants, finding his rock-hard arousal and stroking it.

"*Jesus*. Remind me to read more vampire fiction in future." Tom surrendered.

There was a passion boiling up inside this woman that threatened to overwhelm him, one he was convinced he could match with a passion of his own.

They were both writers, neither had time for social niceties, dating, or any kind of full-time relationship that would fulfill them. They didn't need fulfilling. They wanted to fuck. And write.

Most of the time not in that order, either.

Tom cursed under his breath as he tore at Sally's clothes, and Sally swore as her sweater tangled in her hair.

Neither could get naked fast enough. And God, she was hot.

Not just sexually, but physically. Her body burned as she ripped her clothes away and started on his. A pink flush was spreading over her skin, and her scent filled the room, making Tom dizzy with lust.

She knocked his hands away, impatient with fingers that insisted on unbuttoning buttons instead of wrenching the two halves of his shirt apart.

She had him nude in less than a minute and on the bed a second later.

He bent to her breasts, only to have her hands seize his hair roughly and lift his head. "Don't play nice with me, Tom. It's not what I want."

His eyes watered as she yanked on his scalp. Through the tears that welled in his eyes, Tom could have sworn for a moment her eyes glowed violet, and when she opened her mouth to speak the low light gleamed on something that might possibly have been sharp teeth.

What the fuck?

But then she released him, raised her breast to his mouth and parted her thighs. "Take me. I want you, hard, inside me. Suck me, fuck me, do whatever you want with me."

Tom's cock enthusiastically endorsed her suggestion. Or was it a command? Tom wasn't sure — at this point he didn't really care.

He suckled her nipples, letting his teeth graze the hard buds.

Sally moaned. "More." Heated flesh writhed beneath his, and her fingers dug hard into his back.

Daringly, he nipped her and she cried out. "Oh yessss…"

Her thighs were locking around him, and she was rubbing her naked pussy against his skin, hot liquids branding him from deep inside her.

He pinched her nipples as he slid downwards, noting her little mewls of pleasure. This woman liked it rough, apparently.

He wasn't sure about that, but since he'd reached the apex of her thighs, he figured he'd work that issue out later. After he'd made her come a couple of times.

He bent his head to her cunt, stroking his tongue gently around the swollen folds and licking at her juices.

They boiled, making him jump with the heat that dappled his tongue. "Shit, you're hot." He blew against her skin, cooling it with his breath.

"Fuck me, Tom. *Christ*, I need you to fuck me." Her hands clenched in the linens.

"I'm getting there. Hold your horses."

"I can't. Not this time. I'm ready…too ready." She trembled as he tongued her again. She was ripe, turning to liquid as he sought her cunt. *Fuck.* She really *was* going to come…

* * * * *

Sally knew she'd probably gone over the edge. Dropped off into someplace wild and kinky, driven there by a need the likes

Sahara Kelly

of which she'd never felt before. She ached with the desire to
feel...to have her body claimed by a man. A lover who would
grant her no quarter, permit her to accept nothing less than total
surrender to her passions.

Tom's gentle tongue wasn't doing it.

Oh, he was good, no question. He was a nice guy,
handsome and horny as hell. He was what she thought she'd
wanted, and under other circumstances she'd have been ecstatic
to find him between her legs giving her oral sex.

But not now. Not anymore.

Something was missing. Some edge, some taste—some
sensation was lacking. Sally wanted to come, all right, but she
wanted to explode along with it. There was a place deep inside
her that Tom hadn't touched. And it was that place that
screamed out for release.

Tom was pulling away from her, his face gleaming with her
juices, taut with his own arousal.

Part of her mind registered the condom he opened, and the
nicely swollen cock he sheathed. She panted, ready for his
penetration, ready to climax, ready to...*what*?

She didn't know, but she squirmed and fidgeted, trying to
identify the missing piece of the puzzle. She was hot, hotter than
fire, and the sheets were scraping her back. Her breasts were
swollen and tender, yet not as aroused as she'd hoped. Tom's
delicate pinches had started her on a journey, but she'd not
made it to the first bend in the road.

With a sigh, she rolled over onto her stomach and raised
herself on all fours. Something drove her to present this
submissive stance to Tom.

Who paused. "Uh, Sally?"

"Like this, Tom. Take me like this. It's deeper, harder..."
She wiggled her ass invitingly.

"Okay. I don't want to hurt you, Sal..."

She nearly laughed. *I wish you would.* And in that moment, she realized what was missing. The pain that had lashed at her soul and driven her so much further along into her own arousal. The consistent torture of her body, the visions of her dreams that had made her weep, cry out in her desperate desire, and all but scream with the pleasure of it.

She was becoming that dream woman, that *Suliana*. She needed more than Tom was giving her, simply because she knew there was so much more to be had.

This was scary shit, and for a moment Sally's mind blanked out.

Then Tom slid his cock past her pussy lips, and all the emotions roared back through her in full force.

"Push, Tom. Hard." She thrust her buttocks back into his body, needing him deeper inside her cunt.

He pushed, slapping his balls against the tops of her thighs with the force of it. He touched deep — but not deep enough.

She gasped as he pistoned his hips, hammering her — but not filling her. Wait, that was wrong. He was filling her — not *fulfilling* her. She bit down on her lower lip against a cry of frustration with teeth that seemed oddly sharp tonight. It wasn't Tom's fault...he was a damn fine lover with a cock that knew what to do.

"Tom..." She hissed the word.

"Uh..." He was losing it — *fast*, as he rammed into her again and again.

"Slap me."

Tom stilled, frozen in surprise at her request. "*What*?" His voice was breathless, his muscles shaking against her.

"Slap me. Spank me. Hard. I need — I don't know, just do it, okay?"

She heard his throat move as he swallowed roughly. "Jesus, I don't..."

"Please. Christ, *please* do this."

"I've never…"

"Just do it, Tom. I'm beggin' here…" She writhed, pushing her ass higher and further against him, offering her cheeks. Need ploughed through her, desire shook her to her core, and she shuddered at the mere thought of what he might do.

A light tap on her butt followed. She gritted her teeth, a clash of her jaws that seemed ready to tear into the bedsheets.

"Harder. More. Put some effort into it, for God's sake." Sally's voice was rough now, surprising even herself with its intensity.

"I may hurt—"

"You won't hurt me." She cut his protestations off before they'd begun. "It turns me on. *Do it*, damn you."

Savage me. Ravage me. Send me flying.

A sharper slap followed, a stinging blow that made her blood pound in her ears. "Yessss…more…"

Doing his best, Tom rained blows on her upthrust ass cheeks, timing them with his own thrusts into her heated cunt. Sally panted, short harsh breaths forced from her lungs by the body pounding into her, and the desire rising with each slap.

The sound of his palm meeting her flesh turned her on, and she burned with a furious passion—there was a mountain to be scaled and she was on the way.

But Tom was reaching the peak. And she still had a long trail to climb.

With a cry, Tom hit her hard, a blow that made her shudder and arch her spine with pleasure. *Yes, oh God, yes…this is sooo good.*

For Tom, it was the summit. "Fuuuck…" He buried himself to his balls in her body and exploded, great shaking spasms of release, teasing her cunt as he throbbed and emptied himself.

For Tom, it was done.

For Sally, it had only just begun.

He collapsed over her body, sending her flat to the bed on a sigh of frustration, and struggling to breathe as his lungs heaved against her spine and his hips squashed her belly to the mattress.

"Shit, Sally...I'm sorry..." Tom's voice sounded weakly in her ear and he rolled off her to lie sweaty and limp on his back.

She swallowed and mustered up a grin. "For what?"

The desire that had flooded her was fading fast, the heat cooling from her limbs. The moment had come and gone, and she hadn't. Come, that is. Something had been wrong with it all, some element had been missing.

"Did I hurt you?"

Sally shivered. *Unfortunately no.* "Of course not." She pulled the covers over her chilled body. "You did what I asked, and for that I'm very grateful."

"So it was good for you too? Being spanked like that?" Tom looked hopefully at her.

Sally knew there was only one option. Tom was a nice guy, and a hellaciously fine writer. He was handsome, polite, had a super cock and knew how to use it. He was everything her mother had always hoped she'd bring home.

And he was totally *not* what she wanted.

So she lied. "It was *fabulous.*"

"Really?" Tom looked warily at her. "I've never been into that spanking thing. You get off on that, huh?"

She raised an eyebrow. "It's not a sin, you know. Physiologically speaking, the application of a sharp slap to the buttocks increases the blood flow to the entire genital area. It heightens sensitivity in places that are already aroused with an increased level of capillary expansion."

"Oh." Tom blinked. "Maybe I should take notes."

"Sorry." Sally sat up and looked for her clothes. "I didn't mean to lecture."

"No, no...it's useful information." He stared at her. "What are you doing?"

"Getting dressed." She pulled on her clothes awkwardly as his eyes followed her every move.

"Stay?" He looked longingly at her. "I'd like to do it again."

She smiled and felt the sadness seep into her bones. "Tom, I can't. You know it and I know it."

Sally leaned over and kissed him lightly on the lips. "You're a helluva guy, Tom Silver. And you write extraordinarily fine books. I'm glad we shared…this…" She waved her hand at the rumpled sheets. "But it was strictly a one-nighter. Something we both wanted, both needed, and made us both happy."

Liar. You're a balled-up, fucked-up pile of screaming frustration. She clamped down on her inner voices and walked away from the bed putting every ounce of charm into her smile. "I'm glad I met you. Thanks."

"You're a fascinating woman, Sally Ann Moss. Can I at least call you?" Tom raised a limp hand.

"Next time you're in town? Sure. Why not?"

Sally couldn't get out of there fast enough. She wanted to leave it behind, the emptiness she felt, the lingering gnawing hunger that had gone unsated. But of course she couldn't, since it was part of her soul. It traveled with her as she fled the hotel.

It echoed in her ears along with Tom's goodnights, and thudded in her heart as his door clanged shut behind her.

It was in her head as she drove home, and it gripped the base of her neck as she finally shut herself back into the safety of her own world, her own condo.

It was hovering over her as she stripped, showered, and slid between the cool sheets of her own bed.

She was tired, agonized, and more than a little bit scared.

She knew, without a doubt, that tonight she'd dream. This time, she'd welcome it. Because her dreams were starting to replace her reality.

And wasn't that one scary-as-all-hell thought.

Chapter Eight

I can't move. I can't see.

There was a solid bar of some sort resting across her shoulders and her wrists were shackled to it, her arms outstretched to either side. She was on her knees, thighs pushed apart and held there by something, ankles similarly spread. The softness of the turf cushioned her legs, and cool air swirled around her parted pussy lips.

She was already wet, and the blindfold bound snugly across her eyes merely heightened her arousal.

"Welcome back, my Suliana."

A whisper, a breath of sound—no more than that, and she knew *he* was there. *The Master.*

"I missed you." Hands stroked her bared buttocks, gentle at first, then squeezing and pulling them apart. "I missed your scent." Hard fingers played around her tight opening, then dropped lower, smearing her hot honey over her flesh. "I missed the delightful sight of you like this, so ready for me." Sharp teeth sank into her ass cheek and she gasped. "I missed the taste of you."

Her clit ached as his mouth sucked her blood, then pulsed as his tongue healed the wound.

"So hot. So sweet. So ready for fucking." He had moved away, she knew. Left her bereft and needy. Again.

How long would he do this? How long would he deny her his cock, the mad pleasure of fucking him?

"As long as it takes." His answer wafted around her head, accompanied by a low and husky laugh. "You will be the one to tell me when the time is right."

Her head jerked up, but she could not as yet voice her words. Perhaps she didn't need to. He was reading her so clearly.

"You haven't been trying hard enough, Suli." His voice hardened now. "You must try — *try* with everything you possess."

There was a sudden whoosh behind her and Suliana choked back a scream as a lash landed squarely across her backside.

"You cannot find pleasure elsewhere. Only with me…"

Again the lash cracked, and she felt the drips of blood as they oozed from the welt. His lips touched her, he licked and sucked and healed her.

Only to repeat it all over again.

The lashes stung, the pain shooting pleasure through her to her clit. She wept, tears soaking the blindfold and liquid soaking her thighs. Once more the lash landed, softer this time, just flicking across her skin.

"*Aahhhh…*"

"Good, Suli. Speak to me. Cry out for me. Beg me to fuck you." The Master cracked the lash once more, this time making sure the tip cruelly flicked her clit.

She screamed, filling her lungs and letting the sound force its way past the obstruction in her throat.

"Yesss…" He was behind her, arms around her, cupping and squeezing her breasts with fingers that groped and found her nipples as his teeth sank into her shoulder.

His cock thrust against her anus, and she spasmed at the touch, willing him to force himself into her welcoming heat. She boiled, from the mouth on her neck to the cock against her ass. A volcano trembling on the brink of explosion.

More. She wanted *more*.

He knew. He drank then withdrew, once again sealing the wound. His lips traced the weals on her buttocks, healing those too. "So fiery, my love." His breath dusted her sensitive skin. "So hot."

So angry. Why would he not just take her? Drive her over the edge?

"Not yet."

God-fucking-damn him to hell and back.

"You can go higher. You must go higher. And when you reach the heights..." He paused, then moved away from her body.

She bit back a sob of frustration and moaned. "*What then?*"

He laughed. "You will know."

Know? Know what? Know when? Suliana's mind roiled, fighting with itself. Part of her recognized his voice, knew him for the Master. Another part hungered, frustrated past all bearing. And yet another part, the one belonging to a sleeping human woman, writhed and yearned for the unfamiliar passion of pain.

"You will know when you are whole, my Suli. If you can withstand the Glade of Arraho, you will become whole. And you will know."

Suliana shook her head, cursing the blindfold. She wanted to see him, to look into his eyes as he made his pronouncements in such a lighthearted tone. To watch him as he lashed her with his whip. To see if he was as aroused as she was.

She wanted to see his face, his body, his cock. Above all, she wanted to see his cock, wet with her body's juices, plunging into her cunt as he took her. Claimed her for his own. She wanted to feed from him, draw his life force into herself as she drew his cock into the darkness between her legs. And she wanted him to feed from her as well.

"But for now..." The Master was in front of her. She could feel the heat radiating from his body onto hers. "For now, we shall play."

Sahara Kelly

Her nipples were pinched and pulled, tugged until her breasts stretched away from her chest. The small pain was nothing compared to the savage clamp of the objects he fastened to the hard peaks.

Metal teeth bit into her areolas, sharp things dangled to her belly, and a fire burned an internal trail from her rapidly numbing skin to her cunt. She barely even registered the sting of the Master's fangs as he gently pierced a nipple.

"Mmm." He suckled her, licking around the clamp, his tongue driving heat into her breast, his lips taking blood from her and savoring it. She could hear his sighs of pleasure and her whole body shook.

Her fangs were distended, sharp points against her lips. She hungered.

And as always, he knew. "Talot has requested to be your *Tapa-hir*." The Master paused, then tugged on one of the chains dangling from a nipple.

She sucked in a sob. "I hear you, Master."

"Good. Shall we see if he is strong enough to bear the burdens of that position?"

Tapa-hir. Right-hand man. Liegeman, bondsman, servant and so much more.

The words were familiar, yet strange. Once again, Suliana moved her head, trying to order her thoughts. Trying to grasp that part of her brain that failed to recognize the idea of a body-servant.

She knew what a *Tapa-hir* was. How could she?

"Talot. You may approach." The Master was standing in front of her, and his cock would be close—oh-so close. Suliana let her tongue slick down her fangs, scenting him. How she would love to taste him. To suck from him and heal him, over and over again. To make him come in her mouth, her throat, and then mix his come with his blood and drain him even as he ripped her open to her orgasm.

She squirmed.

Hands touched her from behind. *Talot*. She recognized his scent. Light, needy and pleasant, yet weak when compared to the essence of the man in front of her.

"Talot, do you declare your willingness to become the *Tapahir* of Suliana?"

"I do, Master."

"And you will forgo your own *Arraho* whilst holding that position?"

"I will."

The Master's palm stroked Suliana's cheek and she leaned against it for a brief moment. "He will never feed from you, my Suli. He may take *Tapaha* with you, and you with him. But never — *ever* — will you share *Arraho*. That right is mine, and mine alone."

The Master's hand hardened and Suliana felt her chin grasped firmly as he pulled her jaws apart. A metal ring was forced beneath her fangs, holding her mouth wide open.

She felt the saliva drip from her lips but was helpless to lick it away.

Bound and helpless, nipples numb, cunt empty and clit aching, Suliana cursed the day she was born, and delighted in the pain. Confused and aroused, she moaned. It was all she could do.

* * * * *

Keirat fought for control.

Having Suliana tethered before him, mouth wide open and legs splayed, was playing havoc with his emotions. He wanted to fuck her, rip her flesh from her body, drink from her and then do it all over again. For uncounted years, for uncounted times.

He needed to drain his heart, his blood and his seed into her, and he needed it badly. If she didn't choose soon, he was doomed.

But she was making progress. She was prepared to accept a *Tapa-hir*. Enough of her consciousness seemed to be returning to understand what that meant.

Perhaps — perhaps he could ease his longings just a little as she and Talot bonded in the age-old ritual of Mistress and servant.

"Talot. Proceed."

He saw the shimmer of excitement as it passed over Suliana's skin. She shifted a little, moving her knees, straining against her bonds. She was so hot, so ready. And yet she had not fully returned to him.

Talot knelt behind her and began to stroke her spine. "With each touch I bind myself to your service, Mistress."

Keirat neared her, letting his cock thrust hungrily toward her opened mouth.

"With each caress you accept me into your service, Mistress." Talot scrunched forward, and Keirat knew his cock would now be pressing between Suliana's ass cheeks.

She flinched as Talot found the tight ring of muscles.

"By accepting my cock, you accept me. By penetrating you I give you my allegiance." Talot's hips flexed as he pushed himself forward.

Suliana gasped and shuddered.

Keirat closed his eyes for a second, envying young Talot with every fiber of his being. He wanted *his* cock inside her ass. *His* cock seeking the hot tight darkness within this woman.

His fangs ached with the yearning to rip her open and feed at the same time. Talot's fangs were out, dripping pink fluid, but he had himself under control. This was an honor, Keirat knew, and one that Talot would not take lightly.

It was a good choice. Talot was loyal, intelligent, and likely to protect Suliana with his life should the need arise. He was also a lusty man, with a healthy need for a good fuck. His control was legendary, and if there was anyone Keirat could trust not to feed from Suliana, Talot was the one.

Keirat saw no need to tell either of them that the occasion would not arise. Not in his lifetime.

Other than this one binding ritual, Noul Keirat would make damned sure no other cock *ever* touched his mate.

He was *Master*. She was *Mistress*. It would be so.

Carefully he grasped his cock and slipped it between Suliana's fangs, past the ring gag and into her mouth.

* * * * *

At last.

Something was filling her emptiness, swelling within her to meet the desires that flooded her.

And as it did, something entered her mouth, hard and velvety smooth, sliding past the fangs, the ring and just touching her tongue.

Her ass was opening, relaxing, to allow Talot's cock entrance. Nerve endings shrieked with glee, her nipples throbbed painfully within the restrictive clamps and she shook, dizzy from the invasive presence.

When the Master's cock entered her mouth, Suliana wanted to scream with the joy of it.

Talot pushed harder, into her darkest places, easing himself within, and squeezing her buttocks as he did so.

She welcomed him, consciously angling her hips for his penetration, enjoying the slide of his cock into her body.

But she welcomed the Master's swollen length more. She wanted to swallow him whole. To devour him, suck him dry and make him shudder even as she shuddered. Her fangs leaked furiously, dripping liquids onto her breasts that did nothing to cool the heated flesh.

The Master was teasing her — and possibly himself.

Her shoulders strained against her bonds, wrists pulling taut within their shackles. She wanted to touch him, to bury her nails into his ass and pull him down her throat. She wanted to rip his thighs open and feel his blood pour over her as she drank him, to bury her fangs into his soft sac as she sucked him into orgasm.

The twin assaults drove her insane with lust. With desires unnamed, with needs unformed.

She cried out around the cock in her mouth and squirmed her ass onto the one behind her. It was a violent thing, this desire that burned inside her.

Her tongue sought the ridges and valleys of the Master's cock, flicking madly within the cavern of her mouth, yet always unable to reach the true sweetness of him. A bubble of his come leaked from the tip and she lapped at it like a hungry she-wolf quenching her thirst in a tiny raindrop.

It was not enough. It would never be enough.

She heard him laugh—a strained sound, as he withdrew, teased her tongue then thrust in once more.

Talot panted behind her, sunk to his balls now, a hot presence that stimulated her spine and stretched her deep inside. She loved the feeling. Welcomed it with all that she was. But it was not enough.

It would never be enough until it was *him*.

At that moment, Suliana had no need of the blindfold. She was blinded by her passion, her desires, her hunger.

"Talot…" The Master's voice was hoarse as she frantically wrapped her tongue around every bit of his cock she could reach.

Talot's hands crept around her body as he pressed himself into her as far as he could. "Yessss…Master…*Mistress Suliana*…I surrender. *Tapa-hir…*" Eager hands fumbled at her breasts for the clamps and with one swift move Talot ripped them from her nipples.

Suliana screamed, the pain almost unbearable, the pleasure beyond belief. Talot exploded within her ass, a swelling and throbbing that drove her higher than she could have imagined, her desire choking her with a red haze that sent flames shooting over her shivering flesh.

And the Master came, sighing as he did so, pulling back, just letting his cock spurt hot jets into her mouth.

Sweet and unique, male and powerful, his come spilled down her throat and Suliana eagerly gulped, taking what she could of him into her body. She was a mass of pain and pleasure and need, her clit pulsing between her legs, the one part of her body that neither man had touched.

Once again she was to be denied her own pleasure.

"Oh please...*please...when?*" Cries of anguish formed in her throat, muffled by the gag and the Master's cock.

"Soon my love. Soon. You *will* choose soon."

* * * * *

Shoulders on fire from the agony of her restraints, Sally Ann Moss screamed herself awake, shuddering once more on the brink of an orgasm, the taste of the Master still fresh in her mouth.

She turned to the bedside table. The flower was there, but budded this time, a long black length of furled petals.

Desperately she grabbed it. The petals moved, hardened, congealed into the shape of the Master's cock. She felt it writhing in her grasp, heating as she held it tight.

Without a second thought she parted her thighs, pulled up her nightgown and thrust it deep into her cunt.

It burned like acid, expanded within her, and she screamed once more as the unaccustomed pain shot her over the brink into a maelstrom of sensation that threatened to blow the top of her head off.

She orgasmed, time and time again, going from one peak to the next with hardly any lessening of the tremors shaking her.

It was fire and hell and unlike any earthly experience she'd ever imagined having. And it was ultimately satisfying, sending her to the place she knew existed, a vortex of cataclysmic internal contractions that ripped her soul apart.

And reunited it.

She was Suliana.

Suliana was *her*.

The knowledge washed over her as the shudders subsided, and the flower faded from earthly existence.

Sally lay limply in her bed, two of her own fingers in her cunt, feeling the aftershocks ripple through her muscles.

It was enough but not enough. It was insane, but in an odd way the sanest she'd been in years.

It was, above all, terrifying.

She was two people, yet she was one person.

She was, without a doubt, going completely and utterly mad.

Chapter Nine

From that time on, Sally wrote as if possessed. Which, on occasion, she truly believed she was.

The sense of having a limited time left to enjoy the freedom to create her stories grew stronger by the day, and she ripped through *The Women*, re-reading it, correcting it, saving it and emailing the manuscript to Julie within a mere week of her latest dream.

She appended a note that succinctly said she, Sally, was *fine*, not to worry, and that Tom was indeed very handsome. No sex manual would be forthcoming, however.

There was a decided grin on her face as she wondered what Julie would think of *The Challenge*. When it came to sex manuals, this one had 'em all beat. Literally and figuratively.

The emotions, the savagery of the vampires, the sexual lust—it was all there. And although her readers would never know, it was all written from experience.

An experience she had had, was having, and would stay with her, as part of her brain, forever. Or however long she had left.

The feeling of urgency built, driving Sally into a frenzy of creation, chapter after chapter flying from her keyboard onto her screen. Someone, something—was coming. Quite possibly polite young men in nice, clean white coats. With a straitjacket. Into which they'd lace her before she became too dangerous.

She stopped herself from checking her teeth ten times a day. She did *not* have fangs. Had never *had* fangs. Merely dreaming that she had them didn't make it so.

She faced the fact that she could well be headed into degenerative schizophrenia and madness, a lifetime of drooling into oatmeal and pushing colored blocks around a table. It was frightening, but unrealistic.

Somehow, somewhere, a future lay ahead for her. But it wouldn't be in an asylum. That assurance grew as she neared the end of her story.

She had no more ideas, no more characters knocking about inside her head. For the first time in her life, her idea cupboard was bare.

And yet she was not afraid. For there would be something to replace it. There would be a change, a reorganization in her thought processes, maybe—Sally didn't know. She accepted her conviction that something new was about to arrive in her life. Something that would change it forever.

So S.A. Moss wrapped up her last *Scars of the Lash* novel, and finally typed "The End", without a tear or a regret. She'd adored the world she'd found in the darkest places of her mind. She'd been driven to write about them, people them with such lustfully ferocious vampires, and thrilled to find that readers had devoured the tales with equal fervor.

This particular story was her swan song. Her last term in office, as it were. Of course, only she knew there would be no more *Scars* tales. But this one effectively wrapped up several loose story arcs and surpassed the others with its erotically charged scenes of bondage and torture.

A little something for everyone, mused Sally, as she ran her spell-checker for the third time and made a few minor corrections. Formatting was a chore, but accomplished with the relative ease of familiarity. Title pages were affixed, acknowledgements appended, and the business end of producing a manuscript was wrapped up in a speedy and effective manner.

Sally checked her email. It was a bad habit she'd gotten into, but she took periodic breaks from her writing to see what was up, if anything. Mostly it was suggestions she refinance her house, increase her breast size, maintain bigger erections for a longer period of time or watch pink teen sluts sucking each other off. Occasionally she was invited to participate in a study relating to shopping habits, or purchase a super-expensive watch for less than the price of a cup of coffee.

Just about everything got automatically deleted, but on the afternoon she finished her book, one email in particular caught her attention.

"Dear Ms. Moss."

Hmm. It had come through her website. Most of those went to the publisher, but somehow this person had scrabbled around and found her personal address. She paused, with her finger over the delete key, and let her eyes skim the words.

"...love your work. We'd like to invite you to visit our new nightclub, The Blood Flower. As you may have guessed, it features entertainment of a distinct style, which we think might appeal to you."

Sally's hand froze. *Blood Flower*. It was one of *his* names for her. A chill ran up her spine as she clearly recalled his voice whispering the endearment over her ragingly aroused body.

She read on, the rest of the email containing addresses, an exhortation to her to restrict the contained information to those over twenty-one years old, and a pass, which she was instructed to print out and bring with her should she choose to attend. Toys, it was stated, would be furnished by the club, but she should feel free to bring her own if so desired.

She blinked and re-read the email. Twice.

The more she read, the more certain she became. This was a message. For her. From...whom?

There was no signature. Just the name of the club in elegant script, and a link to the page promising the pass. Sally clicked on it, curious to see what their website contained.

And her heart stopped beating when the page loaded.

It was there.

The flower. The black flower that had haunted her since the dreams had begun.

A simple but classic pen-and-ink sketch of a unique flower, its oddly shaped petals fanned out in full bloom around a stem littered with sharp thorns that looked amazingly like fangs.

She hurried to print the page, watching as the illustration took shape on the pristine white paper. Her pulse thudded in her ears as she read the address and the polite invitation.

"Admit one Guest."

Three little words. And a step down a road to her dreams — or her nightmares. She wasn't sure which.

But she knew damn well she was going to take that step. She would visit this club. If nothing else, it would be interesting from a research point of view.

A little voice inside her head whispered that it might be a whole lot more.

* * * * *

She wore black. There really wasn't much choice, since what else would one wear to a club like this?

Sally closed her door behind her without a blink, drove the few miles to the outskirts of town and parked in the quiet lot. She checked her pass just to make sure she was at the right place.

It was a house, rather than a business. An old house, Victorian in architecture, but contemporary in infrastructure, since there was an automatically triggered outside lighting system and a complex keyboard next to the heavy door rather than a keyhole.

Fortunately, there was also a bell. She pushed it and within seconds was admitted into a tastefully furnished foyer where she presented her pass to the young woman within.

"Welcome, Ms. Moss. We're glad you're here. Would you care for drinks? They're being served in the library."

All politeness, the girl led her respectfully to a set of half-open double doors and the muted sound of conversation that rumbled behind them.

Curious now, Sally walked into the room, not quite sure what to expect inside.

A small group of well-dressed people mingled comfortably in the large room. Bookshelves soared to the high ceiling and the writer in Sally drooled at the sight. There was a lot in the way of old English leather chairs, dark wood and even a fireplace. Somebody had clearly taken a stately home as their decorating mantra and re-created some historic monarch's reading room.

It was lovely and Sally immediately felt at home.

"Wine?" A waiter appeared at her elbow with a tray. "It's our finest...I think you might enjoy it." He smiled.

Sally nodded and took the glass. It sparkled in the subtle lighting and weighed heavy in her hands. Definitely lead crystal.

"Excuse me." A man stood beside her. "Do forgive my curiosity, but aren't you S.A. Moss?"

Sally was surprised. "Yes, as a matter of fact, I am. How did you know? I'm not the most recognizable writer in the world..."

"You are to me. I adore your books. I was at the last 'Bits and Bites' Convention. You received the Golden Fang award for your latest, I think?"

Sally smiled. "How nice. Thank you. Yes, I did."

They chatted companionably for a few moments, Sally relaxing as she realized this wasn't a fan who would demand her signature, a photo and an autographed copy of her latest novel when it was released.

Instead, he was a scholarly gentleman whose interest was intense, and his conversation both challenged and delighted Sally.

She nearly jumped when a hand touched her arm and the young woman from the hall attracted her attention.

"My apologies, Ms. Moss. May I take you away for a moment or two?" She lowered her eyes respectfully.

"Uh…sure." Sally drained her glass and excused herself to her admirer.

"This way, please." The girl led her to one side of the room where writing tables nestled snugly in small alcoves.

One was empty save for a large leather folder, embossed with the flower logo. *Shit. I'm getting the check already? After one glass of wine?*

"If you wouldn't mind…" The girl pulled out the chair and motioned for Sally to sit. "We have a short questionnaire that will help us maximize your entertainment this evening."

"Oh. Well, sure." Sally blinked. She had to take a frickin' *test*? And she hadn't studied for it either.

Another glass of wine appeared at her elbow. "Take your time." The girl smiled and left her alone.

Extremely curious now, Sally opened the folder to find a pen and one sheet of paper. Once again the black flower stared up at her and her vision blurred for a moment, the red wine in the glass flashing maroon beneath the desk lamp and the words on the paper dancing before her eyes.

She shook her head to clear it. *Stupid stuff. Must be the wine.* It was good, though. Strong and rich, not too sweet and with a smoothly satisfying aftertaste.

She sipped and read over the questionnaire.

The first few questions were simple. "What is your favorite color?" "Do you have a favorite fragrance?" "Are you involved in a committed relationship at the moment?"

That she could handle. She reached for the pen. "*Purple.*" "*Anything floral.*" "*No.*"

The next section pertained to work environments, and she gladly followed the instructions at the top. "If you are not employed in a management position, or work independently, please bypass these questions and move to Question 9."

This was easier than her tax forms. Sally moved to Question 9.

"Sexual preference." Hmm. Sally's pen found and circled *Heterosexual*.

"Favorite sexual position." No problem there. *All of them.*

"Frequency of climax — please answer in percentages." *Shit. I knew I should've studied.*

She thought about that one. Well, perhaps honesty was the best answer. *45%*. She wrinkled her nose but let the answer stand.

"Do you masturbate?" *Yes.*

"Do you use toys?" *Yes.*

"Do you fantasize during masturbation?" *Yes.*

"Do you find fantasies of punishment arousing?" *Yes.*

"Have you ever been spanked during a sexual encounter?" *Yes.*

"Have you ever spanked your partner during a sexual encounter?" *No.*

"If your answer to Q.17 above was 'no', would you like to?" Sally chewed the tip of the pen before answering that one. Would she like to be on the giving end? Up to now she'd dreamed of taking a shitload of punishment at the hands of others. And yeah, something inside her told her it was time to turn the tables.

She swiftly wrote her answer. *Yes.*

The next section asked pertinent questions about health issues, covered a few legal matters, and she moved quickly through them, signing her name at the bottom of the page where indicated.

She had accepted their terms. Told them enough about herself to paint a rough picture of who she was and what she wanted. Statistically, she'd probably also opened herself up to a bunch of junk mail she'd spend the next three years throwing away.

She shrugged. What the hell. It didn't matter. Crazy people didn't get junk mail.

She noticed a final optional question. "Are you troubled by your dreams?"

Well, hell. That was the understatement of the year. She unhesitatingly checked off the "Yes" box with a firm hand.

"Thank you." A voice sounded across the table.

Sally glanced up, not even realizing that she was no longer alone. A woman sat there, smiling at her. Elegant and sleek, she had to be the wrong side of forty, but she had that ageless quality that some women possess. Finely honed cheekbones spoke of some European heritage, and her eyes were an unusual shade of blue, ringed by a darker purple line rimming her irises.

"I...uh...you're welcome." Sally sat, as always a little at a loss as to how to best handle the situation. She so wasn't at home with social niceties.

"I'm Adella. I own this establishment. Your questionnaire is vital to your enjoyment. As long as you were honest in your responses."

The blue eyes stared at her, unblinking and intense. Sally shifted. "I was. I have no reason to lie."

"Good." Adella relaxed slightly, sliding the leather folder from Sally's side of the table over to her own. "We appreciate your forthrightness."

Sally smiled. "There's a word you don't hear in conversation too often."

Adella smiled back. "Then you've been conversing with the wrong people." She glanced around. "Here, you'll find lawyers, physicians, ascetics and academicians. We don't cater to the young Goth crowd, or the thrill-seekers. We're serious about our fun."

Sally grinned. "An oxymoron."

"I think you'll enjoy it, oxymoron or not." Adella's laugh was infectious and Sally sipped her wine again, liking the companionable atmosphere that had enveloped the two of them.

"So. What happens now?" Unable to rein in her curiosity, Sally had to ask the question.

"Now, you enjoy your wine, and indulge in some intelligent conversation. Maybe taste a little of our delectable Brie assortment." Adella nodded at a gleaming sideboard covered with platters. "Then…" She paused.

"Nice dramatic pause there." Sally chuckled.

"Thank you. I like it." Adella chuckled in her turn. "Then a slave will take you to your room for the evening."

Too well-versed in the world of BDSM to question the usage of the word "slave", Sally merely inclined her head. "I see."

"And after that…it's up to you."

"Ah."

"Ms. Moss. Your whims, your wants, your needs and your desires…we shall fulfill them all." Adella's voice turned serious. "But you must *let go*. Leave your inhibitions and preconceived notions at the door of your room. Enter with a clear mind and a single goal. Pleasure. The choice is yours. Choose to find your pleasure or choose to hold back. We can only provide the means, not the results. Those, you must achieve by yourself."

"Okay." Sally thoughtfully watched her wine glowing within the crystal goblet. "I think I can do that."

"Good." Adella rose. "You will be summoned." She nodded at Sally and left.

Chapter Ten

The room was at the very end of a long corridor, and Sally's feet made no sound as she followed the "slave". Luxurious carpeting cushioned her steps, muted lighting softened the old wooden walls, and her heart started to thud as the girl opened the door.

"Your room, Ms. Moss. We hope you enjoy your visit."

She was gone in silence and Sally stepped over the threshold, closing the door behind her.

For a moment she thought the room was empty. Tall ceilings soared above her, heavily beamed. The walls were paneled, some places featuring dark smoky glass rather than oak sections.

It was dazzling in a spooky sort of way, especially given that the lights in the room were radiating a soft purple hue.

Sally's eyes shifted within their sockets, adjusting, refocusing, almost changing as she took it all in. It was…familiar, somehow.

Then a young man rose from a chair at the far end. "Good evening, Mistress." He stood, head lowered, waiting for her to approach.

Sally moved closer, looking at him, considering him. He was tall, nicely built, and wearing a simple white shirt unbuttoned over dark slacks. His feet were bare.

"Good evening." What was the protocol for a situation like this? Sally had no clue. But she tingled anyway. This was…*interesting*.

"May I undress for you?" His question was directed at the floor.

"By all means." Sally wasn't about to refuse him permission to strip. That was what she was here for, after all.

He efficiently removed his clothing, folding it neatly and putting it behind him on a chair.

Mmm. Sally's mouth watered. He was quite lovely. A firm chest, well-sculpted muscles, not too hard, solid thighs and a cock that was already half aroused and emerging from the nest of curly hair between his thighs.

"With your permission…" He nodded to one side of the room.

Sally glanced over and blinked at the chains hanging from the bar. "Er…sure."

He strode to the wrist restraints and easily slid his hands into them, securing one and looking at her as he lifted the other arm. "Mistress…I will require your assistance with this one."

She joined him, reaching upwards and sliding the securing pin through the appropriate loops. Her breasts brushed his chest and she sucked in a breath at his muted gasp.

"Your touch. It is…it is most pleasant." He lowered his eyes once more.

"What's your name?" Sally walked around him, studying him. His back was smooth of hair, his buttocks dimpled and hard. He was, in a word, yummy. And he was all hers. A nice toy indeed.

"My name?"

"Yes. I need to know your name."

"T-T-Taylor, Mistress." He stuttered slightly, making Sally smile.

"Don't be nervous, Taylor. I won't hurt you."

Taylor shivered a little. "I'm not nervous about that, Mistress. Quite the opposite. I'm rather hoping you will." His cock lengthened noticeably.

"I see." Sally gave in to temptation and ran her hand over his ass. Yep. Very nice indeed.

Experimentally, she gave it a soft tap.

Taylor sighed. "Oh Mistress…yes please."

She slapped him again, harder this time, leaving an imprint of her hand on his cheek.

Once more he responded with evident pleasure, arching his spine and pushing his ass toward her, a mute appeal for more.

Sally felt the heat sweep through her body and sweat began to bead on her forehead. Instinctively she stripped off her black shirt and tossed it away, pulling her pants, shoes and socks off as well.

The air in the room was warm against her skin. It felt good, liberating and she quickly slid from her bra. *Now* she could play.

She brushed her bare nipples against Taylor's spine and followed it with a hard smack. The sound of her palm against his flesh was exciting and her body responded, her arousal beginning to bloom wetly and soak the thin silk of her panties.

Another slap, another moan of pleasure and they were flooded. With an exclamation of impatience, Sally stripped them away.

Nude now, she circled Taylor, who was biting his lip and sighing with delight. His arm muscles must have been sore, stretched as they were above his head, but his expression told her how much he was enjoying this.

"Anything, Mistress. You may do anything to me." He answered her question before she asked it.

Well, that was nice. A blank slate, *carte blanche* to do whatever she wanted with and to this nice young man. *And they said there wasn't a Santa Claus.*

"Thank you, Taylor. I will endeavor to meet your expectations."

For a moment, he looked horrified. "Oh *no*, Mistress. It is I who must fulfill your expectations. Submit to your will. *Not* the other way around."

"Right. Sorry. Ignore that." Sally blushed. It was hard thinking of herself as the dominant one.

For a split second an ache crossed her shoulders. The ache caused by the stretch of a bar and the lashing of her wrists.

She paused, struggling for the memory.

But it had gone.

She returned to Taylor. His cock was fully distended, and she reached for it, smoothing the skin up and down the length of it and then cradling the balls in their soft sac beneath.

"It is your choice, Mistress." His words were soft, and Sally glanced up at his face, surprised to see a spark of something violet flash across his eyes.

Must be those lighting effects.

"There are tools on the table." Taylor indicated a small alcove by a tip of his head. "You may choose to use any of them if you so desire."

Heedless of her nudity, Sally strolled over to see an assortment of whips, floggers and paddles laid out neatly on a small wooden surface. There were also condoms, some nasty-looking clamp things, ropes, a first aid kit and bottled water.

There was one that looked familiar. Probably one she'd seen online at one of her BDSM research sites.

The beautifully braided leather handle ended in a cascade of short leather thongs, close to a dozen of them probably. She picked it up, finding it fit into her grasp quite naturally. She swished it and caught herself accidentally on the thigh, the small sting stimulating her from eyebrows to heels.

Whoa.

Yeah. This was her toy of choice.

"You like pain, Taylor?" She turned to him, flogger dangling loosely from her fingers.

"Oh yes, Mistress. Oh *yes*." His gaze burned hotly, once more flicking with that odd violet spark.

She blinked. He looked *so* familiar when the light hit him right.

"Then we must see what we can do."

* * * * *

"Taylor" hung by his wrists, a nervous wreck. He was unfamiliar with the environment, although familiar with his position.

His was a mission of the utmost importance—to the Master, to the people of Raheen, and most of all to the Mistress. The woman he had pledged himself to serve. He still wasn't quite sure how this "transformation", if he could call it that, had been accomplished.

All he knew was that the Master desperately needed his help.

The Mistress had not yet made her choice, and time was growing short.

She had issued *Kyreeha*. The Challenge. If she did not return to fulfill that challenge, the Master's rule would wither rapidly and other factions would arise to seize control.

It was his job to encourage her to make the correct choice. And to make it *now*, while there was still time. He had been ready.

He took his vow seriously. His life was now hers, to do with as she would. And if he could get her to do the right things here in this strange world, then perhaps she would be able to make the right choice. To return to Raheen where she belonged.

But in the meantime, she was circling him, flicking her whip, playing with the tails and generally making him nervous.

And aroused.

He had to bite down on the lust, control his desire and his needs. Somehow he had to reach the Mistress buried inside this woman. Bring her to the surface, force her to make the choice to return.

To the Master. To him. And to Raheen.

As he watched her, he wondered if he was up to the task.

She was unique, there was no doubt about it. Although she had light hair, not silver, the firm jaw was all Mistress Suliana. Her eyes were lighter in shade here than they would be on Raheen, but the purple shadows lurked beneath the surface.

He rather missed the fangs, but realized they were not part of the physique of this world, rather an aberration. He clamped his lips together, hoping his own fangs didn't decide to emerge at an inappropriate moment.

She lashed out at him, catching him across the meat of his buttocks.

"*Great ray…*" The expression leapt unbidden from his lips as he writhed in pleasure. She'd caught him by surprise.

He focused on her and her actions, dragging his mind away from his assignment and into the room with his Mistress.

There was a puzzled frown on her face as she circled him once more, flicking here and there with the ends of the whip. "That phrase…" Her eyes met his. For one tiny instant recognition flared, only to die almost immediately.

Her jaw firmed. Staring into his face, she brought the thongs of the whip up between his legs, catching his balls fair and square.

"*Aaahhhh…*" He threw back his head and gasped. Such exquisite pain. Such heady agony, racking him from his head to the tip of his cock.

He was hard as granite, aching to explode, and desperate for more of her punishment. And he had to drive her along the same path. Help her free that part of her that was Suliana, his Mistress.

"Good, so good Mistress…" He let his head droop forward a little. "More. Please give me more. I need it so badly…"

She obliged. Without a word she lashed him, catching his balls, his cock, and then higher, flicking his nipples cruelly and even landing a blow or two in his armpits. Her aim was unerring, her technique superb.

"Taylor" was beside himself. Talot gritted his teeth and hung on.

Somehow he had to reach her. Somehow he had to force her into making her choice.

Somehow he had to unlock the vessel that was Sally Ann Moss, free Suliana and bring her home.

To Raheen.

* * * * *

Sally was confused. She lashed into Taylor with a passion that surprised her and a skill that overwhelmed her. The flogger felt right, she knew by some instinct how to wield it and by doing so she was notching her own responses up, step by step.

She dropped the flogger and reached for a single-lashed whip. "More you shall have. Can you take it?"

He nodded, silently moving his body, asking without words for whatever she chose to do to him.

One crack of the whip and another piece of her brain shifted into gear.

She caught him across his ass, leaving a bright red welt behind. She felt no remorse, no concern. She felt…*hot*.

Her cunt was twitching, leaking liquids profusely over her thighs. Her breasts felt every brush of the air as she swung her arm, and she ached for something, although she couldn't put a name to it.

She was hotter than hell, getting more aroused by the minute, and his cock was looking bigger and better all the time. She loved the sound of the lash as it whistled through the air, to land with a wonderful thud on the body before her.

It was comforting, soothing, oddly familiar and erotic to the max.

Sally realized she was losing herself.

And she didn't care.

Another crack and the welt across Taylor's back split open, slow drips of blood oozing from the wound.

Sally's mouth watered and her teeth ached. She watched, fascinated, as her own hand rose to touch the hot liquid.

Dark blood, richly scented — she could smell it, breathe it in, almost taste it. She *wanted* to taste it. Involuntarily her lips peeled back in a snarl and for a second she felt the pressure of fangs within her gums.

Absurd. But the hunger remained. The need remained. And the desire rose higher.

Her clit throbbed now, pulsing with her heart, beating in tempo with the thunder of her own blood as it raced through her veins.

She lashed again and again, raising welts, bringing more blood, making Taylor cry out and urge her onwards, upwards, toward something — somewhere —

She rounded him, leaving his back bloody and gleaming darkly under the purple lights.

His cock was huge, swollen and reddened, and leaking fluids from the slit. His head was thrown back and his eyes closed as he gasped for breath.

He was teetering on the edge of orgasm, and Sally shuddered with her own desire, a living thing that was exploding inside her. The control she had, the punishment she'd administered, the toys…it was all familiar, all arousing, all…part of who she was.

But who was she?

Jumbled and chaotic thoughts clashed in her brain, warring with the furiously violent arousal she was experiencing.

She reached down and grasped Taylor's cock. "You want to come, don't you?"

The words were hissed between her lips, past gums that ached, over a tongue that thirsted for his taste — his blood.

"If it is your pleasure, Mistress. If you *choose* to make it so." He was hissing too, and Sally caught the glint of purple light on his teeth. His long teeth.

She smiled. *Yesssss.*

Tossing the whip away she squeezed him cruelly. "You shall come. As will I. We shall come together, Tal-T-Taylor…"

"I cannot come within your body, Mistress. It is forbidden." His cry was anguished as she squeezed him and dragged the silky skin up and down his cock.

"I know that, *Tapa-hir*. I know that well."

Huh? Where had that come from?

Sally didn't know. This was a ride that was out of her control. Her actions were slipping away from her, her brain was shaking, her body was on fire, and she was *losing* it. Losing something in her head—but finding something else.

Her free hand slid between her thighs and found her clit. She touched herself, slicking her own moisture over her hot skin. In a concert of skilled moves, she masturbated herself and Taylor, face to face, chest to breast, cock to pussy.

She wanted him in her cunt, wanted to be stretched and filled, but she knew it was forbidden. How she knew, she had no idea.

What shook Sally to her core was her desperate need to bury her face in Taylor's chest and *bite*. The higher she crept toward orgasm, the greater the desire for his flesh. The more natural such a thing seemed.

Her body ached now, on fire from her own touch and the panting breaths of the man hanging so close before her. He was nearly at his peak too, face flushed, lips parted in a snarl of lust, and eyes wide, watching her hand as she worked her clit and her cunt into a frenzy.

Her hunger burgeoned, and she opened her mouth wide. Tingles began low in her spine, presaging the ultimate explosion.

"Talot…" She called the name from a throat that was hers no longer.

"Mistress." He screamed as his cock began to twitch violently in her grasp. "Mistress. *Choose.*"

"Choose what?" Sally fought for understanding. Fought to retain her thoughts, her being, and fought to hold off the orgasm that even now was sweeping to its peak.

"Mistress Suliana. Choose." He cried out again, the name—the name that she knew so well—as he erupted into her hand.

It all fell into place. The dreams. The flower. Raheen. Who she was and who she should be.

She exploded into an orgasm that sent her screaming to her knees, racked with massive shudders of pleasure. She must choose. So much depended on it.

With her hand rammed into her cunt and the spasms of her own climax wrenching the air from her lungs, she struggled for breath.

And found it in her soul.

"I choose. I am Suliana. I must come home. Now."

Chapter Eleven

"Today the literary world mourns the loss of a popular author. Vampire writer S.A. Moss passed away a week ago, apparently from natural causes. The Medical Examiner has ruled that Ms. Moss succumbed to a cerebral aneurysm while walking to her car, and her death was immediate."

Julie brushed the tears from her eyes and shook out the Sunday newspaper. There was more.

"S.A. Moss has written many novels in the vampire genre, which have thrilled and entertained millions. Her latest book soared up the best-seller list, to remain there for weeks. Her contributions to the field will be missed by many. Already her titles, especially those with her signature, are appearing in online auctions…"

A wry grin curved Julie's lips. She knew there were two more novels in the pipeline, to be published posthumously. And wouldn't *that* enthrall fans. Especially since Julie knew they were Sally's best work ever.

She sighed. It wasn't fair. Life wasn't fair. Sally should still be around, quietly buried in her own private paradise of eroticism and lust.

Instead, her ashes had been scattered over the hills she'd so loved to watch from her bathroom window. The ceremony had been small, emotional, and what Sally wanted. A detailed request had been found amongst her papers.

For an author who lost herself in the worlds she created, Sally had possessed a pretty damn solid practical streak too.

Julie stared out of her own window. There were no green hills outside, just buildings and more buildings. She didn't see them. She saw Sally.

Her infectious laugh, her ridiculously opulent bathroom, her passion for her writing and her characters. And the occasional flashes of pain and confusion of late, when those dreams had begun to scare her.

Julie shook her head. *I should've done more. Been there for her.* But it was too late. Recriminations and hindsight wouldn't help ease the pain of such a loss.

She looked again at the small card she'd found in an envelope with her name on it. Sally's mother had given it to her at the funeral, but she'd waited until she was alone to open it, fearing she'd get all weepy again if she read its contents in public.

It was a drawing. A simple pen and ink rendition of a flower. One Julie had never seen before.

And underneath, in flowing script, the words "*I have chosen*".

There were odd symbols along the bottom, indecipherable to Julie no matter how she turned them. Her eyes filled with tears again and for a second the symbols moved, rearranged themselves into a word...

Suliana.

Part Two

Suliana

Chapter One

She was cold. Colder than she could ever imagine being. Chilled to her core, throat practically frozen, with icy shivers running over her body as she moved a little against something equally cold and hard beneath her.

"*Suliana*. My Suli. Come back to me, *please…*"

It was a whisper of sound that forced its way past her hair and into her ears, to end up wherever such sounds were registered and interpreted. It took its own sweet time, too. She breathed slowly, in and out, in and out, as life trickled back into her body.

She knew that voice. It resounded through her limbs, finding a home in her heart, where it awoke a sleeping volcano of emotions. For a moment she tumbled helplessly in a vortex of confusion, then her world settled down. She was home.

And her Master was waiting for her. Her mind filled with joy and excitement, part of her relishing the familiarity of her mate, the other part thrilled and overwhelmed at the notion of the real Raheen.

The *real* Master.

The two parts became a whole, a Raheen soul blending with a spark of humanity into something new, something unexpected. And something shivering.

"She's here. She's *back…*" There was that voice again, accompanied this time by a hand to her face. A heated palm stroked her cheek, her neck and down to her naked breasts. A tiny sensation between her eyebrows was the best she could do for a frown.

Angry words simmered — "*Back off, buster.*"

She neither understood them nor had the strength to utter them, but they were there, nevertheless. Rattling around in her head with other strange thoughts. Purple skies, two moons, fangs and blood — all things that Suliana found comforting. But coupled to these were brief glimpses of blue skies, a yellow sun and a strange room that gleamed with clear water and plants.

Suliana sighed.

Beyond anything, she craved warmth. Else she would surely die on this cold, hard surface.

Forcing her strength upwards and focusing her energies on one small set of muscles, she slowly opened her eyes.

"*Yessss.*" It was a howl of triumph that rocked the room.

She stared, blinking a little to clear the blurriness from her vision.

He was there. Bending over her, touching her, and reaching for a blanket of some soft stuff that he began shrouding her with, wrapping her tightly.

It was heaven. And so was he.

Eyes of the darkest purple stared down into hers. Little maroon lights flamed behind the pupils as she gazed at him. His face was strong, lines sharply delineated, jaw firm and lips full.

Ink-black hair fell around his shoulders like a puddle of silk, catching the lavender lights in the chamber and reflecting them back tenfold. Some sort of loose robe covered him, black and purple, and for a second Suliana yearned to see what was beneath.

To touch him freely, without restraint. To feel his heat against the chill of her flesh and soak it inside, thawing the frigid and frozen parts of her.

She shivered, shook within his grasp as he lifted her bundled body from the slab and cradled her.

"Get her into the water, Master." The sharp command was rapped out by a woman, and Suliana struggled to move her head in the direction from whence it came.

But there was no time to pursue that movement. He had her swept from the chamber through a doorway and into another room, this one lighter, brighter and filled with steam.

She blinked. *Wow. This is one helluva bathroom.*

A huge sunken tub filled one end with mist rising in pale purple wisps from its surface. Slow bubbles oozed and plopped within it, the liquid a darker lavender and clearly heated.

Suliana yearned once more. But this time for the feel of that liquid around her body. She could hold the man, the *Master*, later. Right now, she wanted that bath.

And, bless all the Gods wherever they were, it looked like she was going to get it.

He carried her to the ledge, dropped to one knee and pulled the blanket away, her weight apparently less than nothing to him. Within moments she was naked, teeth chattering, and then…and then…*bliss*.

Thick waves of liquid heat smothered her, lapped around her and she sank up to her chin as feeling returned to her all-but frozen limbs. She breathed in a soft floral fragrance and felt her lungs expand as the moist warm air crept into the coldest places.

She closed her eyes and spoke for the first time. "Shit. This is *soooo* fucking good."

* * * * *

Noul Keirat, Master of Raheen, blinked.

Those weren't exactly the words he'd expected from the lips of his newly resurrected mate. Nor had he anticipated the sheen of odd colors that flooded her eyes. Granted, in the Glade of Arraho, she'd been barely conscious, a half-presence that had fulfilled the rituals, but only on a psychological level.

Now she was here, home on Raheen, and whole.

And…different to what he'd expected.

Then she groaned, stretched, stared up at him with a slow smile curving her full lips and a bolt of hunger rocked Keirat back on his heels.

Oh *yes. This was his mate.*

His fangs shuddered to life as he reached for her, his whole body suffused with a heat he could not deny. He wouldn't have been surprised if the water had hissed and steamed around his hand as he slipped it beneath the surface and caressed her belly.

The grin widened, her own fangs emerging, slowly at first, then lengthening. Two white knives lying across the redness of her lips. Her eyelids grew heavy.

"Keirat. Noul Keirat. *Master.*"

"Suliana. My Suli. *Mistress.*" His hand moved, creeping over the softness of her body and cupping one full breast.

She sighed. He slid long fingers to her nipple, teasing it, flicking it and then pinching it hard between thumb and forefinger.

"Yessss…" The strangled hiss emerged from her throat along with a moan of pleasure.

Keirat could see the flush of life returning to her skin along with the deepening colors of desire as he aroused her. It was entrancing him, bewitching him, and his cock ached beneath his robes. He wanted to climb into the tub with her, slide himself down her silken body and thrust deep into her cunt at the same instant he sank deeply into her flesh. He wanted to devour her, bring her blood to life and claim it as his own.

And he wanted *her* to want the same thing.

Her thighs parted beneath the surface of the thick liquid, and he knew that there would be more liquids there now…her own…pink-tinged and fragrant. He leaned forward, releasing her breast and sliding his hand back down to the vee of her thighs.

Her pussy lips swelled at his touch, and he parted them, knowing he'd find her treasure lurking in their folds. Her clit, hard and hot, thrust into his grasp. He clutched at it, pulling hard, freeing it from the surrounding skin and squeezing it tightly.

She sobbed out a cry of delight. "Keirat, oh *Keirat…*" Her hips rose as she demanded more of his savage foreplay.

"*Keirat.*" His name sounded loud, echoing around the room and making both him and Suliana jump.

"Behave yourself. There's work to be done before you sate your lusts." The words were sharp and admonishing, coming from a woman who had entered the chamber. She turned and beckoned and a stretcher appeared, bearing the bloody body of someone else…*Talot.*

Oh great ray of light. What had Suliana done to him?

It appeared she was asking herself the same question.

* * * * *

"Oh no…no…*Talot…*" Suliana's voice was still weak, but pain flooded her as she saw the young man's body lying rigid.

"There's still a chance. Move over, woman." Thus reprimanded, Suliana slithered to one side of the tub, making room beside her.

She risked a glance at Talot then raised her eyes. "Will he live?"

The older woman shrugged, and Suliana recognized her in a flash. "*Adella.* You are Adella."

Her words were ignored as the servants helped Adella lower Talot into the water and keep his head afloat. Suliana strained with every ounce of her returning strength, moving to his side and sliding one arm beneath his neck.

"You don't have to do that," Keirat barked at her.

"Yes I do." She snapped back the response. "I did this to him. He's my responsibility. So shut the fuck up while I try to help him."

Silence fell. Suliana ignored it. Stupid rules, stupid protocols. This young man had risked all for her, to bring her home. Keirat should be on his knees thanking him instead of glowering at her from the side of the tub.

A low gurgle of laughter distracted her. It was Adella.

"My, my. The Mistress has learned to use her teeth. And not just her fangs, either." She nodded. "It is fitting. Time we had a Mistress with guts."

Suliana set the issue of guts aside. This was neither the time nor the place. Talot's head lay heavily on her shoulder, and although the warmth of the liquid was now cradling them both, he showed no signs of coming around.

"The liquid will help heal his wounds." Adella's voice was rough as she smoothed the hair back from his face.

"But will it be enough?" Suliana's heart turned over. This was her *Tapa-hir*. Her sworn servant. She had more questions bubbling in her mind than stars in the night sky, but overriding them all was her concern for him.

"I don't know, child." Adella's words were somber. "He's strong. He's always been strong…"

Suliana stared at her. "He's your son, isn't he?"

Adella nodded, eyes full of pain. "Yes."

"And he is my *Tapa-hir*. Together, we shall not fail him." She was resolute, strength pouring through her. "*I* cannot fail him. What kind of Mistress would I be?" She spoke to herself, but her words echoed through the silence.

"You will be *my* Mistress." Keirat grunted.

"I know *that*," Suliana huffed with impatience. "But for right now, don't I owe this man something? He's here because of me. He saved me. He brought me back so that I *could* be your Mistress. It would be a lot more helpful if you had something useful to suggest, instead of acting like a sour-tempered animal."

She turned away from him and back to Talot. "He is too weak. I don't like the look of this at all."

Adella hesitated. "Mistress Suliana, if he were to feed…"

Suliana glanced at Keirat. "Would it work?"

Keirat straightened his shoulders. "Possibly. You know he cannot feed from me. No one but you can feed from me."

Suliana pursed her lips. "Did I ask *you*?" She turned away. "*Men*." Without hesitation, she lifted her wrist to her mouth.

"No, Mistress…you are too weak. Let me…" Adella knelt beside the tub, but Suliana stopped her with a look.

"He may be your son, but he is *my Tapa-hir*. The decision is mine."

She felt the light sting of her own fangs against her skin as she ripped open the pale flesh below her hand. Blood gushed, hot and sweet and familiar. A tremor of desire shook her, and she ached for Keirat in that second.

But Talot needed her. Not for passion, or for sexual fulfillment, but for his very life. Some things simply had to take precedence.

Suliana held her wrist to Talot's mouth and pushed, parting his lips and forcing her bleeding arm within.

For a long moment nothing happened and Suliana held her breath, waiting, watching as small droplets of dark maroon leaked down his face. Then — he moved. Just a twitch, a light brush of his tongue against her wound.

"*Yesss…*" She hissed her pleasure past the fangs that had reemerged at Talot's touch. "He drinks."

"So I see." Keirat squared his shoulders and looked at Adella. "Tend to them. I shall be in my quarters." He spun on his heel and left.

Suliana's gaze met Adella's. The two women shared a moment of purely female communication, then returned their attentions to Talot.

Chapter Two

Adella watched the new Mistress as she prowled Adella's chamber, returning now and again to the low bed where Talot slept, to check on him.

Suliana was not as she had expected. There was a *vitality* to her. An aura of energy and forcefulness that surprised Adella, and had obviously caught Noul Keirat unawares.

Her silver hair tumbled past her shoulders and onto her full breasts, wavy and with a distinct tendency to curl, unlike her predecessors who had been praised for their silken straight locks. She was taller than the norm, too, and in certain lights, her eyes…well, they were different. Other shades flickered amongst the violet of their race, colors that defied description.

She was indeed all that was necessary in a Mistress. But she was, in Adella's opinion, also *more*.

Suliana bent over Talot again, tucking a cover around his frame. "He is healing very quickly now." She straightened and smiled at Adella.

"Indeed he is. Thanks to you."

Incredibly, Suliana blushed. "Hey, I did what I had to do." She shrugged off the compliment. "But I need information, Adella. I need to know what's going on. I feel like…like I've been asleep for a hundred cycles of our moons."

Adella chuckled. "No, only a little over three." She thought for a moment. "That would be about thirty or so of those years on that other planet."

"Hmm." Suliana dropped into a chair and reached for the goblet of refreshing juices that Adella had served. "This is good, by the way."

"Good *for* you too. It'll restore your physiology, strengthen any muscles that have weakened during your time of separation and get you strong again."

Suliana gazed at her. "You are *Matriha*. The advisor to the Mistress."

"I have that honor, yes." Adella dipped her head.

"Then advise me. How did you manage to get me back? How did Talot appear there at the right time? And *why* —"

Adella held up her hand. "So many questions. Stop, Suliana. Breathe. I shall try to answer them, but all in good time."

Where to start? How much to tell? Those unusual eyes remained fixed on Adella's face and the woman sighed. Nothing less than total honesty would do for this one. She knew that with a certainty.

"To answer your last question first...you were brought back because Noul Keirat needs you. Desperately."

She stopped Suliana once again as the younger woman's mouth opened. "Not just for mating. Yes, he needs to take your *Arraho*. When you surrender fully to him he will share in your strength, become complete, and find whatever measure of contentment Masters achieve. But there is more. Much more."

She leaned forward, serious now, intent upon conveying her point. "There is dissent, turmoil, unease amongst our people. They look to the Master for solutions, but without you he has none to offer."

Adella sighed. "Our numbers continue to decline. Our harvests go unreaped, our stores dwindle. In response our women bear fewer children. We are becoming increasingly vulnerable, Suliana, not only to potential invaders, but to disruptions from within."

Suliana nodded. "It makes sense. A strong Master rules with a strong hand."

"Keirat is strong, make no doubt about that. But he is faced with challenges at every turn. More than even he can handle alone. He needs your strength, your presence, and whatever else you bring with you to your mating. Perhaps..." She glanced down at the table, away from that piercing gaze. "Perhaps he needs your wisdom."

Suliana snorted. *"Wisdom?* From *me?* I doubt it."

"Don't. You are more than you think." Adella spoke the words from her heart. "You have brought something of that other one back with you, Suliana. I can sense it. You are different...changed in some way I cannot yet understand."

Suliana frowned. "I don't—"

"Your actions with Talot were completely unexpected. You took control, saved him when you didn't have to. It was...it was as if you knew exactly what you were going to do and did it, regardless of the fact that the Master was standing right there."

Suliana waved it away. "I did what was *right*, Adella. What needed to be done. No more, no less."

"Yes you did." Adella nodded her agreement. "But for the first time, maybe ever, you didn't *ask permission*."

Suliana's mouth gaped. "I was supposed to bloody ask *permission* to save Talot's life? Are you out of your frickin' *mind?*"

"Is that Suliana or the other one speaking?"

There was silence in the room.

* * * * *

"How is the transfer accomplished?" Suliana voiced the question that was uppermost in her thoughts.

"I do not know. That is a mystery lost to time. But essentially, the portion of your spirit that makes you *you* is removed, placed for safekeeping in the soul of another newborn being elsewhere."

"Okay. Go on." Suliana listened intently. She needed to know more than the hazy legends and myths that were familiar to every Raheeni woman.

"We do not know how or why the choice is made. We only know that it is. From that point on, the body rests, and deep in the caverns is a chamber where the locations of the separated spirits are mapped. Lines of light connect Raheen to its Mistresses. When you were chosen by Keirat, your line turned bright...it pulses. I am allowed to visit that chamber as your *Matriha*. I knew where you were."

"And..." Suliana encouraged Adella. She sensed there was more to this situation than was common knowledge.

"When the time of mating nears, the spirit returns to the Mistress. It separates from its...its host, if you will, and returns intact. The Mistress arises, the mating takes place and Raheen survives."

"Yes. This I know." Suliana pursed her lips. "And in my case...it was different?"

Adella nodded. "Yes. You issued the challenge in the Glade. That hasn't been done for uncounted centuries."

"I remember that." Suliana grimaced.

"And your return." Adella looked grim. "Your host did not survive."

"*What?*"

"The woman whose body you shared. When you departed, she died. Or at least her body did." She stared hard at Suliana. "I believe she came with you. Her essence, her spirit, her strength...she was an unusual woman with great intelligence and an amazing drive to create. She was a writer. I believe she *wanted* to come with you. Be a part of you. I think she's here, now, *in* you."

Suliana gulped. "She...I...the times in the Glade..."

"Yes. She was there, much more so than any of them realized. She shared those experiences, wrote about them, yearned for them as much as you. She is you and you are she, Suliana. Get used to it, because I think it has happened for a reason."

Adella rose and moved to the bed as Talot moaned slightly.

Suliana stayed where she was. This was an awful lot to think about. Uppermost in her mind was sadness for the woman who had shared so much with her. Vague impressions of words on a screen, laughter, the pride of accomplishment—all that, Suliana had unwittingly destroyed.

Or had she? Was she now a melding, a blend of two spirits? Or was the whole spirit greater than the two separate parts?

She winced. This was going to give her a stinking headache. "Okay." She tried to organize her thoughts. "So I'm home. I'm here. In Raheen, where I'm supposed to be."

"Yes."

"But you had to come and get me. You and Talot." She frowned at Adella.

"Yes. Like yourself, we did what was necessary." Adella folded her arms. "Your host…did not want to let go. Or something. There was a closer mental bond there, one that you were unable to break on your own. It's odd. I could find no reference to anything like that in our past. Talot and I pretty much took a risk that our plan would work."

"How did you—"

Adella stopped the question. "There are some things even Mistresses may not know. Or Masters." Her face fell into somber lines. "Secrets are entrusted to only a few. Those of us who would serve Raheen and not abuse the knowledge. We will probably go on to become *Rahanarat*, the wise ones, when our time of service to the rules is done."

"Ah, yes. The *Rahanarat*." Suliana nodded at the mention of the select group of senior Raheeni. Ones whose wisdom was unquestioned, and who carefully maintained the history of Raheen. "I should visit them."

Adella pursed her lips. "I'm not sure if you'll be able to."

"Whyever not?" Suliana was shocked. "It's only courteous. And I could use their advice."

"There are only three left."

Suliana gaped and stared at Adella. *"What?"*

Chapter Three

Keirat paced his chambers in a fever of impatience.

He wanted his mate. He wanted to fuck her, feed from her, feel her flesh beneath his whip, his hand, and most of all his cock.

He was getting desperate. Desperate for the ritual that would bind them to each other.

And it wasn't *all* sexual.

He needed her, in a way that only the rulers of Raheen could understand. He needed the strength he would reap from their mating, their feeding, their sharing.

Masters absorbed strength from their Mistresses, and the process worked both ways. Together they were greater than they were individually. It was not fully understood, but the joining of the most powerful with their chosen mate produced a rare blend of both.

It was a mating for life, too. There would be no others for Keirat or for Suliana. He knew that from his feet to his eyebrows. Other rulers had taken *Tapaha* outside of their mates. While the ultimate fuck, the *Arraho*, was reserved for one's chosen partner, *Tapaha* could be taken freely with whomever one pleased.

Keirat did not please. He did not even consider the notion, either for himself or for his Mistress. His cock, his fangs, his very essence was committed to Suliana, and he needed to get a move on with the whole committing business, clear his mind, strengthen his rule and ease his aching cock while he was at it.

Unthinkingly, he flung a small ornament at the wall and watched it shatter with a degree of satisfaction.

The time was near, too near. Suliana had waited until the last possible moment to make her return, and he was damn close to his wits' end. Chanda tormented him whenever they passed, doing her best to arouse him, and when that failed, to taunt him with her version of what the Challenge, the *Kyreeha* Suliana had issued, would lead to.

His ultimate defeat. Chanda's ascension to Mistress with her own Master, probably Kael Melet. He was her partner of choice in the Glade. They had shared *Arraho*. But Keirat admitted that Chanda made him...uncomfortable. There was something in her look that spelled trouble. A deceitfulness, perhaps, a threat, or some kind of cunning. He couldn't put a name to it, but it made the back of his neck itch.

He walked to his desk and riffled the papers lying untidily across it. More reports of poor crops. More complaints that there were no new *Rahanarat* within the ranks of their people.

He snorted and stared out of the window. Why should his people choose a life of learning when they could share *Arraho* in the Glade any time they wished?

He shook his head. Somewhere, something had gone wrong on Raheen. The lives of the Raheeni had swerved from their paths. The desire for sexual gratification and power had overcome the need to survive and thrive.

He wasn't sure if he could correct it. He didn't even know when it had started, or how. Or why. He did know that if he didn't rule strongly and well, Raheen could descend into a state of chaos, something from which they might never recover.

His eyes drifted to the sky, watching clouds forming over the distant mountains. Simultaneously, his hand drifted to his temple, absently massaging the dull headache that plagued him so often these days. Perhaps there would be rain to help the fields limp along and increase this season's harvest. It would be a good omen.

But that circumstance was beyond his control. Suliana, however — *she* was within his control. And if all went well, she would be his tomorrow night. Maybe even sooner. He'd just have to see how well she recovered.

His fangs lengthened a little as he remembered the gleam of her body in the bathtub.

Great ray of light. It's going to be a magnificent Arraho.

* * * * *

The subject of Noul Keirat's *Arraho* with Suliana was on other minds as well.

"The fucking bitch is weak...*aaaaaah*..." Chanda moaned and writhed within the chains holding her flat on the bed.

"So you say."

A leather strap whistled through the air and landed with a thud on a rounded thigh. Melet wielded it carefully, landing sharp, solid slaps exactly where they would do the most good.

"Mmm," Chanda purred. "I'm right. You'll see." She parted her thighs even more, stretching the ankle restraints to their limits. "Melet. Don't stop..."

The pinch of the ringed clamps around her nipples had squeezed them into elongated peaks and the pain brought pink tears of pleasure to Chanda's eyes. She licked her fangs as she watched Melet lean over and suck one deeply into his mouth.

Her body ached with need. How wonderful it was to feel such ravaging desire. And how good Melet was at arousing it. "More, Melet."

His face darkened and he delicately sank one fang into the hardened nub.

"Uhhh..." Chanda's mouth gaped behind her fangs, and her cunt throbbed, responding to the sharp penetration.

He licked the tiny pinprick closed. "A snack. No more. Not yet."

She pouted and lifted her hips in mute appeal. "You're cruel."

"And you want me."

"Oh yes."

"Good." He raised the strap once more, this time catching her high on one thigh, sending a sharp gust of air across her pussy. The sound of leather meeting flesh ricocheted around the room.

Chanda shuddered with pleasure. She could stay like this forever. Trembling beneath the blows, aching for the pain, weeping juices of delight from between her legs to soak the bed beneath. Ready for his cock, his fucking, but desperate to prolong this sensation.

She watched him, his muscles gleaming in the low light of her chamber, flexing as he raised his arm and brought the lash down again and again. Yes, he was good. And he was smart as well. Something she'd not found in previous lovers, no matter how talented they'd been with their whips.

"She waited too long to return. Noul Keirat has too much on his plate for her arrival to make any difference now." Chanda spoke carefully, aware of the desire so close to her throat.

Melet paused, eyes narrowed. "He is not weak. He wouldn't be the Master if he was."

"Agreed. He has risen with much strength and ruled with a firm hand. But he has his vulnerabilities. Suliana is one of them. Take her out of the equation and he is half of what he could have been."

Melet's lips curled cruelly. "So you are suggesting we kill the Mistress?"

"Suggesting?" Chanda closed her eyes and smiled. "Not at all. It isn't a suggestion. I shall kill her myself."

He snorted. "Of course. You will be allowed to quietly slice the Mistress's throat and drain her life from her."

She opened one eye and stared at him. "Do you think I couldn't?"

"Not at all." Melet shook his head. "I know you could. But I also know that permission to do so will not be given."

Chanda closed her eye again and grinned. "I don't need permission. It will happen during the *Kyreeha*."

That statement made Melet pause and wrinkle his brow. "The *Kyreeha*? The Challenge will be met by the Mistress's champion."

"Not if I have anything to say about it." Chanda wriggled her ass against the sheets. "Trust me, Melet. It's time to start a few new traditions. Time to insist that the Mistress meet her own challenge. And I think *this* one will be ready to answer the call."

Melet walked around the bed and stood between Chanda's outspread legs, staring thoughtfully at her pussy. "So you would fight the Mistress. Hand to hand. Whip to whip." He considered the idea. "And without her having shared *Arraho*, she will not have the strength of the Master."

Chanda said nothing.

"You will be able to legitimately win. But will you be able to do more than show her as weak?"

At that, Chanda opened her eyes and raised her chin. "I will kill her. Don't mistake me. I *will* kill her." She lifted her head and stared at Melet. "The Master will be distraught. I shall proclaim him and his choice of mate to be flawed. *You*, my darling Melet, will then administer the fatal blow which will rid Raheen of its current ruler." She smiled and rested her head back down. "At which point, *we*—you and I—shall step into the void our evident strength has created. Nobody would dare oppose us."

She heard Melet chuckle. "Nicely thought out, my love. Very neat. Very tidy." He leaned against the bed, and Chanda sucked in a breath as his fingernails scraped down the inside of her legs. "Do you think you are strong enough to be Mistress?"

She chuckled in her turn. "Yes."

"Let's see."

Chanda tingled all over. She kept her eyes shut deliberately, to heighten the anticipation of what Melet would do next.

There was a slight sound and then her ankles were jerked upwards, roughly, stretched even further apart, and secured.

She panted. Her cunt was spread wide open—she could feel the swollen folds as her position tugged them apart. Without volition a little moan of excitement escaped her throat.

"You like that." It was a statement not a question.

"Yes." The statement was answered in the affirmative, unyielding and intense.

"Good." Melet had moved, and before Chanda could track him, something dark swallowed her head. *The hood.* She shivered delightedly.

Melet pulled the fabric over her face, securing it at her neck. Only her nose was free. The fit was tight, too tight for her to move her mouth. It was restricting and exciting, and Chanda couldn't wait for more. Always more.

She drew in a breath slowly, managing to part her lips enough for the fangs to slide past her lower lip. The thick stuff over her face cushioned their tips, but grew damp as they leaked tears of arousal. He was taking her to the heights tonight.

The thought of being Master…

It turned him on as much as it did her. Power—always power. Without it, one was nothing.

"I have a new plaything. And I think the time is right to try it out." Melet's tone was conversational, but Chanda could hear an undertone of coiled excitement. It resounded within her and she longed to tell him to hurry up. To play. To fuck her, rip her body open, drive her over the brink.

But the hood held her words at bay. She could only wait.

The bed moved as he reached for her, and rough fingers pulled her pussy lips wide, exposing the clit that was now trembling with need. Something cold, hard and sharp slid around it, tightening…more and more until Chanda felt a scream of delight bubbling in her throat.

She moaned beneath the hood as the clamp snapped into place, cruelly pinching her clit, pulling it from her body and sending bolts of painful pleasure through her cunt.

But there was more to come. The clamp moved as Melet adjusted it, and suddenly something hard and cold touched her, slid past her pussy and into her heated darkness. Solid and unyielding, it penetrated her completely, expanding within her passage, filling her to the point of agony.

She howled silently at the intrusion, shudders of arousal electrifying her muscles.

"And now we can play."

She scarcely heard his voice, but she felt the bed dip as his weight settled between her outstretched thighs.

The clamp was connected to the dildo. The further in Melet pushed it, the more it distended her clit. She was being ripped in two, needing the savage pain more than she'd ever needed anything before.

What Mistress could withstand this torture? Was she not fit? Fitter than any other to seize the role of ruler by the throat and show Raheen the true meaning of the word "Mistress"?

Melet activated the intrusive device and it began to move, revolving slowly inside her cunt. The vibration shimmered through her tautly stretched clit as well, and she shook, great trembles of arousal.

Hard fingers dug into her buttocks, lifting her off the bed a little, and she felt Melet's knees slide beneath her.

She was stretched wide, nearly torn apart, and he knew it. He pushed her to her limits and then past them. It was the reason she'd chosen him from all the others. *He knew.*

And his next move proved it. With a sound of sheer joy he thrust his cock between her ass cheeks and deep inside her anus.

Chanda wanted to explode. The hood kept her silent, but her body shrieked at the pleasure and the pain. Her fangs pressed hard into the skin of her lips and her chin, and she struggled, fighting for more. More of this wondrous sensation, more of his cock, more of *anything*…

She knew her wrists were bleeding now, but ignored it as Melet began the slow withdrawal and reentry, fucking her ass with steady strokes, refusing to be hurried or to respond to the screaming need he'd aroused in her.

The dildo vibrated and revolved, her clit felt enormous, her ass expanded to take as much of him as she could, and with the plundering her breasts heated, their clamps biting savagely into the fragile skin of her nipples.

It was pure delight, pure erotic pain, and Chanda greedily took every single drop, relishing the agony, riding the waves of sensual torture, and climbing higher toward her peak.

Once again, Melet proved his worth. Seconds before Chanda exploded beneath him, he tore off her hood, letting her see the length of his fangs, dripping with their juices, splattering drops onto her body.

He snarled, hammering his cock deep into her ass. She snarled back.

It was time, and they both knew it.

Melet lowered his head, finding the side of one full breast. He fumbled with the other nipple, flicking the catch on the metallic ring and releasing it, sending boiling shockwaves of agony through Chanda's body.

It was enough to send her over, and as she shrieked aloud Melet sank his fangs into the soft swell beneath his mouth.

Chanda's vision blurred, the tide of her orgasm swamping her, tearing at her, ripping her apart.

With a groan and a massive effort, she pulled her shoulders off the bed and leaned into Melet. And as she peaked, her cunt savagely clamping down on the dildo, her mouth found warm skin.

She shook with the force of it, every organ screaming its release. She bit down, fangs sharp and hungry, ripping away skin, flesh, muscle…releasing a wave of spicy maroon blood into her mouth.

She fed, suckling frantically, letting the boiling liquid maintain the orgasmic tremors that racked her body.

Melet fed from her, savaging her breast with his fangs, lapping the hot juice that flowed from her wounds, and finally crying out his own climax.

Her ass throbbed as his cock erupted inside her, filling her to overflowing with his semen as he drained her blood from her breast.

She screamed again, the sheer pleasure of sharing this intimately painful act a joy all its own.

Later, much later, when the restraints had been banished, the room tidied and cleaned, and all the wounds healed, Chanda lay next to Melet in a state of contentment. He slept, a sleep he'd truly earned by anybody's standards.

And she smiled.

What a Mistress I shall be.

Chapter Four

"Noul Keirat."

The words came from the doorway to his chamber and froze Keirat into immobility.

"She who would be your Mistress requests permission to pay her respects."

He turned slowly away from his desk and saw her. His Suliana. Standing tall against the darkness of the hall, her hair a silver light, almost blinding him as the rays of the setting sun danced over the soft curls.

She spoke the ritual greeting, the one he'd expected to hear from her lips when she first awoke from her long sleep. But...better late than never, he supposed.

"You may enter." He felt the harshness in his throat, forced the words past a choke of desire. Just the mere sight of her was enough to harden his cock into painful rigidity.

She walked in, looking around her with interest. "Nice place you've got here."

"*We've* got here. These are *our* chambers. The residence of the Master and Mistress. I have lived here alone, Suliana. But now I am ready for you to share it with me." He stared at her closely. "When will you be ready for me?"

Undercurrents of sexual desire flowed around the room, small eddies of heat and need between the two of them. He could feel their swirls as an almost tangible presence, and as she shifted, he realized she could feel them too. His fangs ached a little.

"My *Matriha* recommends a night's rest. Other than that, she tells me I'm fine." Suliana's unique eyes met his, sending him a clear message. *Hands off, for tonight.*

He sighed. "How's Talot?" He turned away, attempting to find distraction in his work.

"Doing better. He's sleeping and his wounds are healing now. Something about the journey to…to…wherever I was prevented our normal healing from taking place. Now that he's home, and he's fed, all will be well."

"That's good." Keirat toyed with a paper. "Talot is a fine young man and will serve you well as *Tapa-hir*. He distinguished himself in our last battle…"

Suliana seated herself and tipped her head to one side. "Tell me. I need to know, Keirat. I need to become familiar with Raheen today, not as it was when I was forced apart from myself."

Her gaze was steady, and quelled some of the sexual desire flaring through Keirat's veins. He took his own seat in the tall chair behind his desk. "I don't know where to start."

Suliana smiled gently. "How about with that battle? Another attempted invasion?"

He nodded. "Ships were detected by our warning beacons. We activated the defense grid. Only a few passed through, and even now we're not sure how. Their fleet was totally destroyed, of course, and we took care of those few who made it to the surface."

"Talot must have been quite young…"

"He was. It was the first time he was old enough to fight for Raheen. He pursued several invaders into the hills and we thought we'd lost him." Keirat grinned. "Then he appeared out of the valleys, bearing the heads of the four aliens."

Suliana sighed. "So savage. That we must destroy to protect what is ours."

Keirat frowned. "Savage? Surely invading another world is a great deal more savage. There have been over twenty such attempts in the last three generations, Suliana. And yet we still survive."

She waved her hand. "I know."

"They come from the skies, from other worlds, to seize what is ours, to destroy who we are, to invade—to conquer—" He stared at her. "What would you have us do?"

Suliana rose and walked to the window. "I cannot answer that question. I know Raheen must and will survive. It is my home. My world." She stared out at the darkening landscape. "And yet..."

"And yet?" Keirat wanted to rise and stand behind her, to look out with her and see what she saw. But he admitted to himself that such close proximity would strain his control. He wasn't sure if he could keep himself in check.

"When was this last battle? I don't remember one since I was a child."

Keirat paused, thinking. "It wasn't that long ago. Perhaps just after you were chosen. I don't recall exactly."

She nodded. "Keirat, what happened to the *Rahanarat*?"

He swallowed, surprised at her swift change of subjects. Her mind was clearly functioning rapidly, absorbing the current state of Raheen in all its intricate confusion. He was impressed. "They passed away. As *Rahanarat* do. Many were of a similar age...it has left us a void, sadly."

"A *void*?" Suliana turned and pierced him with a sharp look from those interesting eyes of hers. "There are only three left, Keirat. *Three*. I remember there being dozens of them."

He could keep his seat no longer. Her lure was too strong to resist. Keirat stood and walked to her, allowing himself the pleasure of resting his hands on her shoulders and turning her back to the window. Great ray of light, she smelled wonderful.

His fingers tightened, noting the little tremor his action produced in her body. "I am Master of Raheen, Suliana. But I have no control over life and death. We are diminished by the loss of the *Rahanarat*. And I certainly could have used their wisdom in the years since then."

She shrugged a little. "I understand. Adella has told me some of what's been happening. I can sense more from what she hasn't told me." She turned then, pulling from his touch and facing him, chin held high. "This is a bad time for Raheen, Keirat. The crops are failing. The birth rate is dropping. The people are discontented and would rather fuck than work to improve matters."

He spun away from her and stalked furiously across the room. "Do you think I don't know that?" He slammed a fist down on his desk. "I have to see it, day after day. The last winter season there were only a handful of children birthed to our women. There was less food stored than ever, so perhaps it wasn't such a bad thing."

He clenched his teeth. "I have tried, Suliana. I have set workers in the fields. We have planted as much seed as we can. But I cannot make it *rain*." He closed his eyes, fearing she would see the pain his admission was causing him. "I cannot stop our people from fucking, Suliana. Nor would I wish to. It's our way. Our tradition. We must preserve it."

"So why aren't they breeding? They're sharing *Arraho*. Feeding from each other. Releasing the eggs to mate with the sperm. It's all part of the process..." Her question fell into silence.

Finally Keirat spread his hands. "I do not know." It was a relief to say those words. Masters seldom had the luxury of admitting their shortcomings. Yet within moments of her arrival, Suliana had him baring his soul. "The *Rahanarat* would have been the logical ones to consult, but they were dying..." He lowered his hands. "I simply do not know."

"I would like to visit those who are left."

Keirat blinked, surprised yet grateful she'd let his admission of weakness pass without comment. "Of course. Whenever you feel strong enough."

Or I let you out of my bed.

* * * * *

The chambers definitely needed a woman's touch, decided Suliana, as she gazed around her. She had many questions cluttering her thoughts, but knew that they must be asked in the right manner at the right time. Keirat might be her mate, but he was also Master.

It was a heavy burden—just *how* heavy she hadn't realized until a few moments ago. "May I see our sleeping quarters?"

Aha. That changed his expression. Nothing like a little sexual innuendo to cheer a man up. "Of course." He politely gestured to an archway at the end of the room. "Through here…" His silk robes swished against his legs as he strode before her and entered, waiting for her to follow him.

She stepped inside and looked curiously at the hallowed sleeping chamber of the Master of Raheen. And his soon-to-be Mistress.

A huge bed dominated one end, covered with red silken fabric and festooned with scarves, leather straps and a few chains…all the trappings of Raheeni sexual pleasure. The walls were bare, though, with just a few stone carvings high up toward the ceiling. Her bare feet sank into something very soft—furry—and she laughed with delight. "Oh my."

He smiled back. "Yes. It's an antique. One of the benefits of being Master."

She looked down at the black pelt, or pelts, rather. There were many of them, interwoven into a carpet that cushioned the stone floor. It must have been a relic of the time when furred creatures roamed free, hunted by Raheeni for their skins and their flesh.

A wry smile curled her lips. "It's strange, isn't it?"

"What, the rug?"

"No." She shook her head. "The fact that we gave up eating flesh so long ago, and yet we devour each other in our...sexual desire."

Suliana kept her gaze lowered to the floor. She could not look at him right at that moment, since she could feel a flood of *exactly* what she was talking about rushing through her skin, heating her blood, and really turning her on.

Involuntarily, she swayed, only to find strong arms around her, lifting her off her feet and carrying her to the bed. "You're still weak."

Well, thank *you*, Captain Obvious. "Probably."

His cock pressed hard against her body as he walked with her and she sighed with regret as he lowered her onto the red covers. "You should rest."

She snorted. "How can I rest?" Suliana swallowed, and released the stranglehold on the emotions uppermost in her mind. "How can I possibly do anything other than look at you? And want you?"

His expression heated, a fire glowing behind his violet eyes. "I know." He took a step toward her, clenched his fist, and stopped. "But we cannot. Not yet. Not until you are strong enough to share the *Arraho* with me." He let his fangs slip free of his lips. "It will not be easy. I desire you with every fiber of my being. And you know it."

"That's how it's supposed to be. With Master and Mistress. We are mated, Keirat. You chose me. You knew I would respond in kind."

"And yet..." Keirat paused. "You are—different. Not quite what I expected."

Suliana raised one eyebrow. "You are disappointed?"

"Great ray, *no*." He glanced down at the cock tenting his soft trousers. "Can't you tell?"

She grinned. "Yeah. I was kind of hoping that was for me." A wave of exhaustion swept her in the wake of her sexual arousal, and she leaned back against the pillows, watching this glorious man. *Her* man. Her Master.

"Keirat…" Her voice was lazy, husky even.

"What?" The cords in his neck were taut as he struggled with himself.

He's gonna break something if this keeps up.

"I have an idea." She wriggled into a comfortable position and toyed with two of the shining ropes that were fastened to the bed.

It was his turn to raise an eyebrow. "Why does that make me nervous?"

Suliana laughed. "Not a clue. But…it could be fun." She felt a definite lick of arousal all the way down to her toenails as he smiled around his fangs, gently teasing her.

They both knew there would be nothing gentle about their mating when the time came.

"So." It was a purr of sensuality. "What did you have in mind?"

Her hands lowered to the ties on her robe. It was a traditional Raheeni Mistress robe, deep in color, flowing from shoulder to floor in a cascade of rich fabric. The sleeves were tight from wrist to elbow, then billowed out, allowing for ease of movement and air circulation when the day was warm.

She began to wriggle out of the garment, taking her time, knowing her every move was being carefully scrutinized by the man at the end of the bed.

One shoulder was bared, then the other, and the sleeve fastenings finally released. She struggled a little with them, but didn't dare ask for assistance. Neither of them wanted that sort of closeness when the cost might be too high.

Freeing the last catch on her gown, Suliana slithered to the edge of the bed and stood, letting it fall to the fur rug around her ankles.

Nude, she stood before him. "I have dreamed of this, Keirat." And how true *that* was. "I have yearned to be this way, with your eyes upon my nakedness." She raised her hands to her breasts and cupped them. "These are yours. All that I am is yours. You have called, and I have chosen to answer. Our destiny lies with each other, with our lives here on Raheen."

Suliana turned back to the bed and lay facedown, her head resting on the soft pillow. "I am told by those who know such things, that I may not yet share *Arraho* with you. And in truth I don't know if I have the strength." She reached out to either side, slipping her hands into the small rope nooses that lay at the edges of the bed.

With one tug she was secured. "But you desire me. And I desire your touch." She moved her hips, letting her ass slide in front of him. "Take *Tapaha* in me, Keirat. Let us begin our lives together with something simple, something pleasurable, and go from there."

Chapter Five

Noul Keirat, Master of Raheen and ruler of most of the damn planet, broke out in a sweat and gulped as he shook like a raw youth.

Suliana's ass was blinding him. He knew what he'd see there if he moved but one step closer. Sweet hot pussy lips, gleaming with her moisture, swelling as her arousal grew. A tight rosebud ring of anal muscles, clenching and then opening, parting for him if he desired to take her that way.

That way? His brain sneered at him. *You want her any way and every way there is.*

He forced himself to straighten, to *not* fling himself onto her shining white body and arouse that pink heat he knew would spread across her skin as he claimed her. "Uhh…"

His fangs slipped free, and the sensation distracted him enough to regain some semblance of control.

"You will not hurt me, I know, Keirat. I want you—you want me. We cannot achieve the ultimate joining yet. Surely we can take some small pleasure in each other?"

How could she sound so logical? So calm? Keirat's eyes feasted on her, and noted a little tremor run through her spine. Hmm. Perhaps she wasn't quite as calm as she wanted to appear.

He hungered. His whole body ached to seize her, penetrate her, devour her. To rip into her body and drink her soul. To become one with her in so many ways he felt dizzy for a moment just thinking about it.

But he must respond. "All right." *Oh great.* Very smooth for someone who was supposed to be in charge of things. He cleared his throat and unbuttoned his own robe.

And a knock sounded on the door.

"Not *now*."

On the bed Suliana jumped as his snarl echoed around the room. And, damn her, he could've sworn he heard her giggle.

The knock came again. "Master." It was Adella's voice.

Suppressing most of the twenty-three curses that were scampering angrily through his brain, Keirat tugged his robe back together and strode away from the bed. "*What?*"

"I have something for the Mistress."

He flung the heavy wooden door open and glared through the opening at Adella. "What?"

"You're repeating yourself." She glared right back at him.

Great ray of light. Doesn't anyone respect the Master any more?

"My apologies. Suliana is resting. What was it you wanted?"

Adella's expression was polite and amused. He obviously wasn't hiding much of anything. "I have a drink for her. It will help her relax and build her strength." She glanced down at the distorted pants and back up to his face again. "Perhaps you'd like some too?"

Keirat swallowed. He could do this. He could refrain from killing Adella on the spot. She had only the best intentions for Suliana, after all. As did he himself. The *very* best intentions.

"I will see she drinks it. My thanks." He began to close the door. "Oh, how's Talot?"

Adella's smile widened. "Doing well. Thank you for asking." She nodded her head. "I shall see that you are not disturbed for the rest of the evening."

Keirat raised one eyebrow. "That will be *much* appreciated."

"Master?" Adella's voice was stern. "Do not exhaust her. You cannot feed from her yet…"

"I know." He ran one hand through his hair and blew out a harsh breath. "Believe me, I know."

"Sheathe those fangs and *perhaps* I'll believe you." Adella grinned and walked away.

Keirat closed the door and carried the drink over to the bed. "Adella says you should drink this. It will help you relax."

Suliana turned toward him. Yes, she had been stifling her laughter in the pillow. "That was too funny for words."

"Right. Are you going to drink this?" His hands were already stripping away his clothing.

"Keirat, only one thing will relax me right now." She licked her lips as her fangs protruded a little. "*Your touch.*"

The Master was lost.

* * * * *

Suliana ached.

Her muscles were tired, struggling with the activity that had returned to them after the long sleep. She knew her physical abilities were limited. But that knowledge did nothing to soothe the ache that permeated her soul for the man standing so close to her.

It was as if she had been ripped from *him*, not just Raheen. She needed to join with him. To reinsert herself into him and have him return the favor. They were two parts of a whole that had been torn apart for too long.

She wanted him. She wanted to fuck him, taste him, feel his body cover hers. She wanted the sting of pain he could give her, the sensual torture only he could provide...she desired all these things with a passion that was physical in its agony.

But they would have to wait. The genuine exhaustion was not to be denied. Right now, she was offering all that she was capable of, and praying he'd accept.

It would have to suffice them both, for this night anyway.

And as the bed dipped, she closed her eyes and sighed with anticipation. He was going to play. With her.

Oh yeah.

"Ahh, Suli…" Strong hands swept a path up her legs from her heels to her buttocks, and she quaked, glad now that her arms were restrained. One touch, one caress and she was ready to jump him, savage him and take anything he could dish out.

Or at least thought she was.

She closed her eyes, imagining his beautiful body, his cock, every part of him. She heard his robe fall to the floor and felt the heat from his skin as he knelt on the bed so close to her. But not close enough. It could never be close enough.

Her legs were pushed apart, and his knees slid between them in the space he'd created. She tried to close her thighs, to trap him, hold him against her.

But he would not permit it. Within seconds, her ankles had been tied, held where they were. She was comfortably spread-eagled on her stomach, resting her body and yet presenting it for his pleasure. She fought against the restraint a little, but then relaxed into it.

This time it did not presage the onslaught of wildly erotic savagery or magnificent pain-filled ecstasy. But it did mean he was going to touch her.

And touch her, he did.

With delicate precision, a pair of fangs ran gently along the length of her spine, sending tingling delight across her skin. They lifted, only to be replaced by the weight of his body as he rubbed himself over her, letting his cock fall heavily against her ass.

"Mmmm. Keirat…so good. So warm." Suliana's eyelids felt heavy, and her fangs emerged, slowly and softly making their presence known against her lips.

"Yes, my Suli. Oh yes." His weight disappeared, but his hands lingered, massaging her back, kneading her muscles and eventually squeezing her buttocks. "So sweet."

She sighed as his hands gave way to his tongue, a heated wetness searing her ass in a semicircle from the top of one thigh all the way to the little sensitive spot at the base of her spine and down the other side. "You can taste me, Keirat…"

Please. Taste me. Make me bleed with the desire you're arousing.

"I know. But I shall not. You drive me mad, Suli, but I have enough control for the both of us." His cock touched her once more. "I *think*…"

She smiled, her fangs dripping now onto the pillow beneath her cheek. "I weep tears of passion for you, Keirat."

His cock snuggled between her legs, moving around her pussy lips, teasing other moisture from her body. "So I see." The bed jiggled as he moved, sliding himself slowly up and down the cleft of her buttocks.

"Ahhh…" It was heaven and hell for Suliana. Her Raheen nature cried out for the savagely sensual fulfillment of a true mating. But a part of her relished the unusual tenderness, the time Keirat was taking to arouse her, and the teasingly erotic experience of being splayed and restrained for his pleasure.

And hers.

He teased her body, kissed her flesh, licked the backs of her knees and always returned to bathe the head of his cock in the warmth and wetness that bloomed between her thighs.

She moaned as its silken steel spread her cheeks apart and the damp head pressed the muscled ring between. "Oh yes, yes…"

Suliana's wrists pulled against the ropes, her body tightening now with a need for Keirat to plunder her. Her exhaustion was forgotten, replaced by adrenaline—and lust. "Take your *Tapaha*, Keirat. Share that with me. *Please*…"

"I will. Be patient, little one. My blood flower. I want to see your skin blush for me." He slipped a hand between her legs. "I want to feel your cunt cry for me even more."

"It cries, Keirat. I can hear it. My pussy is on fire for you. I have thought of nothing but fucking you, sharing *Arraho* with

137

you, for so long…" Suliana let her words tell Keirat what her body could not.

"I cannot tell you how the waiting is killing me. I desire so much from you. I want the sting of your lash. I want to bleed for you, and make you bleed in return. I want the pain only you can give me, and the passion that will follow. I want the heights and the depths of you, Keirat." She pierced the pillow, biting down in her frustration.

"You shall have it." His voice was deep, his cock pushing harder now between her ass cheeks.

The swollen head throbbed with his pulse as he began to force his way inward, past the tight muscles. She trembled with pleasure, willing her body to open for him, to accept him, to take him within. "Yesss…"

"I could've killed Talot when he took you like this in the Glade…" It was a hiss of agony and pleasure, ripped from Keirat's throat. "I wanted to savage him. Destroy him for having what I could not."

"I remember." Suliana closed her eyes. "But I cannot remember *Talot*. I only remember *you*. Your cock. In my mouth. I wanted to swallow you, suck you dry, take you into my throat and never lose the taste of you. In that moment there was nothing else…but *you*." Her fists clenched into the bedclothes as his heat filled her.

"And I wanted that too. I wanted your lips around me, not that damn ring gag. I wanted your teeth against my cock, my balls against your face. I wanted to fuck your mouth until we were both blind from the pleasure of it."

He moved, slowly at first, pulling back and then easing his way deeper, stroking her buttocks, letting his sac brush against her pussy as it swung with his strokes. "There is so much I want, Suliana. So much I need."

"I know." Suliana gasped out the words, suffused with heat, with arousal and with desire for her mate. She trembled, her weakness betraying her.

Keirat reached for her, gripping her hips. "I take my *Tapaha* with you, Suliana. But only for tonight. I thank you for this gift."

His cock plundered now, each thrust a pleasure, an ache in her ass and her body that rippled through her cunt like a wave of boiling passion. She welcomed it, needed it, and wanted more.

"Ahh, Suli…"

She felt the drips of liquid from his fangs on her back and nearly cried out with delight as his length swelled even harder, ravaging her ass, and he dug his fingernails sharply into the flesh of her hips.

"Suli…*Suleeeee*…" He froze for long moments, buried to the hilt inside her darkest places.

Then he exploded.

And Suliana cried out for him, a shriek of joy at the pleasure of finally being filled by her Master.

Pulsing eruptions of his seed burned her, flooding her with pleasure and his passion. He seemed to hold time still, keep it at bay and at the mercy of his *Tapaha*. Long breaths of timeless delight, long moments of sheer and simple happiness.

For both of them.

Gently Keirat withdrew, easing his cock from her body and releasing the pent-up juices to flow in a warm stream over her skin. His hand stroked them, blending them on her flesh with her own moisture.

"The two of us, Suliana. Our essences mixed, indistinguishable." There was awe in his voice. "Amazing."

The breath snagged in Suliana's lungs at the sound of his words. Tenderness, delight, passion…all there. If she'd had any doubts about her destiny with this man, they would have vanished as he spoke.

But she'd had none whatsoever. Tonight had simply reaffirmed that she was in the right place. *With the right Master.*

She surrendered to her exhaustion as Keirat released her bonds. Her eyelids closed, and she slept.

Chapter Six

Noul Keirat was smiling to himself as he slid behind his desk the next morning.

He'd left his mate snuffling quietly into her pillow, although it had been extraordinarily hard to peel himself away from her body. He was satisfied on a very minimal level, but at least it was *something*…it would have to tide him over until they could fully explore the passion he knew burned between them.

She would never know how hard it had been for him not to rip into her, drink from her, feed the hunger that only she could arouse to such heights. But he'd done it, distracted by the feel of her, the smell of her, the incredible fuck they'd shared — without the blood.

Today she was to visit the *Rahanarat*, a short trip, but one that would take her away from his residence for a few hours. And that was probably a good thing, since he needed to get some work done without the ache of an erection that zoomed to full strength whenever Suliana was near.

His cock stirred. Make that when he even *thought* about her.

Her strength was returning, the Challenge would be met and dealt with, and then they could share their *Arraho*. Raheen would have a settled ruler, a good Mistress, and — with any luck — rain.

And sure enough, he was hard and pulsing with need just from the thought of *Arraho* and Suliana.

Keirat shook his head at himself. Some things apparently even Masters couldn't control.

He forced his attention to his papers and away from his silver-haired enchantress.

There were the usual complaints, legal matters, land ownership disputes, and crop reports. He went straight to the last ones, since the failure of so many of their crops was one of his major headaches.

And speaking of headaches, Keirat realized he didn't have one this morning. Probably a byproduct of his *Tapaha* with Suliana. He reread the page in his hand.

Fuck. Yet another field had failed to germinate correctly. This was the fourth in a row.

By now, the grain should've been sprouting, stretching delicate fronds to the sky. But it wasn't happening. The lack of rain was a serious problem, certainly, but they'd increased the amount of irrigation from their wells. It should have helped, should have increased the survival of the plantings, but clearly it hadn't.

Keirat glanced automatically out of the window, hoping— as he did every single day—to see great purple clusters of rain clouds. But—as he had done every single day—he saw a clear sky. The watery sunlight flooded the plains unobstructed, and dappled the mountains in the distance.

Raheen was a small planet. And its population was getting smaller all the time. They had half a year to provide for themselves, store sufficient food to see them through the long harsh time when their orbit took them far away from whatever warmth their small sun provided.

The other planets in their system had fared better, orbitally speaking, maintaining a more constant temperature. But Raheen's orbit had put them in a unique position. Keirat knew his world traversed more of the planetary system than the others, a scientific fact that produced its extreme climate. And also put them in an excellent position to launch explorations out past their local region into other areas of space.

The farthest point of their orbit took Raheen to the very fringes of the system, and made it most desirable for other species who would have liked nothing more than to make Raheen a staging area for galactic travel.

And the Raheeni would have none of it. They had no intentions of becoming a space outpost. They were who they were, unique, savage, and fiercely protective of their planet and their traditions.

Keirat sighed. The shields were functioning, but their technology had stagnated over the centuries. And recently, without the guiding hands of the *Rahanarat*, there'd been no advancements on that front at all.

The *balance* of Raheen had shifted. Toppled into an unhealthy place from which they'd be lucky to emerge unscathed. If they survived at all.

He shuffled more papers, reading a few, signing others, discarding more. One caught his attention—a small slip, unsigned.

Keirat frowned. This wasn't an official document...it was a handwritten note.

"Chanda intends to challenge your Mistress. Personally. Be warned."

He turned it over, turned it back, and read it again. The message was unmistakable. Chanda was going to use the *Kyreeha* ceremony to kill Suliana. Why the hell she'd issued the damn challenge in the first place, he had no idea. It was seldom done, hadn't been called for a few hundred years, and implied a doubt in the mind of either party, Master or Mistress.

Did Suli have doubts? It did not appear so. Not after last night. Not after what she'd said, what they'd done.

Keirat pinched the bridge of his nose and thought it through. Traditionally, a *Kyreeha* was answered by a Champion. He'd assumed it would be him, and he would face the choice of his people—most likely Kael Melet or one of his cronies. It was their way. It ensured the strongest ruled.

And he knew *he* could take Melet or anyone else, for that matter. But Suliana?

Chanda was within her rights to step forward and answer the *Kyreeha* on her own behalf. It was rare, but there were no rules barring women participating in such a ritual.

The entire process was part and parcel of who they were. Strength, might, the ability to defeat the weaker in battle, all these characteristics had made for a history of solid and indefatigable leaders, Masters who could handle not only Raheeni, but the invaders that besieged them. It was harsh, but it worked. Especially for a race that depended upon savagery, erotically charged savagery, to survive and breed.

Keirat rose and paced the floor. The *Kyreeha* would take place the following day, according to their tradition. But would it be soon enough for Suliana to triumph? Could she *possibly* defeat Chanda? He knew the answer. And he didn't like it.

He also didn't like the only option that was presenting itself. If this note was real, and all Keirat's instincts were screaming at him that it was, then Suliana needed strength. *His* strength. The strength she would gain by sharing *Arraho* with him.

The *Arraho* that wasn't supposed to take place until *after* the challenge. Until the *Kyreeha* had been met and fulfilled.

To save his Mistress, Keirat was going to have to consider violating his own people's rules. He was going to have to take *Arraho* with Suliana earlier than he should. Break with tradition, throw all the centuries of ritual to the winds, and seduce her into letting him fuck her blind, then feed on her as she fed on him. He hoped she was strong enough, prayed her body would withstand the incredible stresses she'd encounter. He knew he had no choice.

The worst part of it all was the guilty realization that he couldn't *wait*.

* * * * *

Suliana had awoken to her first full day on Raheen, full of energy, a little stiff and sore, but none the worse for her night with Keirat. In fact, she hungered for him, missed him when she realized her bed was empty, and ached to see him.

But she knew he had duties, as did she.

Her trip to visit the remaining *Rahanarat* was first on her list of things to do. If she was going to rule this planet alongside Keirat, and do a good job of it, she needed information, clear and accurate information. And probably also the guidance of these wise people, even though there were only three of them left.

That fact still shook her to her core, and it was with a somewhat apprehensive step that she left their home and ventured out toward the distant compound where the *Rahanarat* had lived for uncounted generations. Her vehicle was waiting, a driver at the ready to help her inside. The solar-powered drive was silent, and she got her first good look around as they covered the miles across the wide plain.

The state of the crops was self-evident. Where there should have been fields of grain, there was dust. No young shoots springing freely into the air, no flowers, even the trees seemed sparse and poorly leaved.

Signs of drought were everywhere, and Suliana frowned as she recalled the much lusher and more vibrant home of her youth. She narrowed her eyes and squinted into the distance. Drought happened. Part of her consciousness recognized this fact and accepted it. It had happened before and would happen again.

It was why there was a cluster of shiny bubbles in the far reaches of the valley. Large protective shields covering the complex well and irrigation system that contained the vital liquids needed to sustain Raheen and its people during such times.

It appeared intact, at least from where Suliana was sitting. She wondered if it was worth detouring to check on it, but then remembered that the *Rahanarat* would have the current water level status, along with all the other pertinent information she needed.

Only *three* of them. How the hell had that happened?

Her brain roiled at the thought. She was seeing Raheen through eyes that recognized so much and yet found it all new, all unfamiliar. Like the words of an old song that had been set to a new melody. It was strange, but somehow refreshing.

Suliana felt her consciousness expand, soaking in the sights and sounds of Raheen and sorting through them with an efficiency and a curiosity that enhanced her understanding.

The vehicle drew to a halt in front of the large gate to the complex housing the *Rahanarat*. Ancient walls protected them, but instead of the buzz of activity, there was a silence that chilled her.

Alone, she stepped from the carriage and pushed open the massive door. An answering creak echoed from within the compound as a face appeared. "Welcome, Mistress." A hand waved, beckoning her to the darkness of the first building.

Thank the great ray of light. Somebody was at home.

She walked into the quiet building. "Greetings to the *Rahanarat*. From Suliana." She bowed her head respectfully.

"Forget that nonsense. Get in here." A harsh voice answered her formal words.

She blinked. An elderly man was leaning on a stick, frowning irritably at her and pointing at the room behind him. "Get into the laboratory. Quick, woman."

"Yes, Oh Revered One." She followed him.

A snort shook the old man's frame. "Nothing revered about me anymore. I'm Parnulet. Just an old man." He cackled. "With things to tell you now you've finally decided to get your sweet ass over here."

Suliana choked back a laugh. "I came at the earliest moment, sir."

He snorted again. "Right. Damn near the last possible moment, if you ask me."

"Which she didn't, you old crow." Another voice chimed in, softer and more melodious. Suliana turned to see an old woman, slender and still elegant, move quietly into the room to join them.

"My apologies for Parnulet, Mistress Suliana. He's a cantankerous bastard these days."

Suliana gaped. "Great ray of light. I *know* you. You are Nupira."

"I have that honor." The woman inclined her head.

Suliana bowed. "Your poetry was an inspiration. Your words were…magnificent."

"So were her tits." Parnulet chuckled to himself. "Always wished I could do something about gravity."

Nupira rolled her eyes and indicated that Suliana should sit. "Ignore him. His brains are still functioning, believe it or not, even though his cock isn't. And *that* particular impairment drives him crazy most of the time."

"Hah. Don't you believe it, girlie…"

"Not *now*, Parnulet. There are urgent matters to discuss."

Parnulet subsided, muttering, in front of his data console. "Got as good a cock as any of these young squirts…"

Nupira followed her own advice and ignored him. "It is good that you are here, Suliana. You know that there are only three of us left."

Suliana nodded. "I was horrified when Adella told me, Madam. What happened? Why are there so few of you?"

Nupira sighed. "There is much you do not know. And even more we are not sure of. There is so little time…"

"Then let's not waste it." The last of the remaining *Rahanarat* walked in and closed the door behind him. "Hello, Suliana."

Her jaw dropped. "*Father?*"

Chapter Seven

Sorl Dralet stared at his daughter. How lovely she was. What a woman, and what a fine Mistress she would make.

Of course, the gapingly idiotic expression on her face right at this moment didn't exactly betray the depths of her intelligence.

"*Father?*"

This time the word was a squeak. He sighed. "Yes, Suli. It's me. Now, if you please, let's get past the familial relationship and on to business."

"But...but..." She swallowed awkwardly. "I never knew you were going to become *Rahanarat*. I always thought you'd..."

"Fuck myself to death?" He chuckled as she colored.

"Er...well...something like that, yes."

Nupira coughed back a laugh. "Becoming *Rahanarat* doesn't mean giving up much of anything, Suliana. It simply means that we accept more knowledge, actively seek it, and are prepared to run with whatever we find." She smiled at Suliana. "We still fuck." A wry grimace crossed her face. "Or we used to, anyway."

"Some of us still do," Parnulet mumbled over his console.

"Well, shit. You're sure blowing a number of my illusions to hell and back." Suliana stood and paced the room, ending up in front of Dralet. "Okay. So my father is now *Rahanarat*. I'll get over it. Tell me what the fuck is going on?" She glanced around. "Er...pardon the informality."

Dralet stared at her. Her eyes, liquid pools of intermixed colors, shifting with her emotions and quite unlike the ones he remembered from her youth.

He shot a quick look at Nupira. She nodded back. She had seen them, as well.

"Sit, Suli." He pushed her back into her chair. "There are only three of us. We're working as hard as we can. But there is grave trouble, a serious threat, and we don't know if we are up to the task of saving Raheen."

"Saving Raheen? It's *that* bad?"

Dralet watched the color fade from her cheeks. "Yes, daughter. It's that bad." He sighed. "To start with, the *Rahanarat* didn't die from old age."

Suliana's fingers gripped the arms of her chair. "Are you trying to tell me they were killed?"

Nupira intervened. "In a way. They were—aging. As are we. We are the youngest ones left. When our elders began to sicken and pass away we assumed it was simply their time. Now we have our doubts."

"Why?"

Great ray, she went straight to the heart of the matter, this daughter of his. Dralet took up the tale. "One or two things. Firstly a large number passed away within days of each other. That was unusual. Then our death rituals started picking up...abnormalities."

Suliana thought for a moment. "The processing of their blood."

It was customary on Raheen for the blood of a dead Raheeni to be drained and offered to the land in tribute. It was an honor, and the blood of the *Rahanarat* was particularly revered, being scattered into the finest fields.

"Yes. Damned old coots." Parnulet interjected his mite into the conversation. "The processor went phlooey."

Nupira sighed. "By 'phlooey', Parnulet is attempting to explain that sensors detected abnormalities. It has taken us a long time to identify them."

"And you have?" Suliana leaned forward. "You have found what it is?"

Dralet nodded somberly. "Yes. A bacteria. A foreign and completely new bacteria in their blood."

"Good grief." Suliana blinked. "Like a virus?"

"In a way. It works in the bloodstream, silently attacking various parts of the brain. We have yet to understand exactly how. There aren't a large number of volunteers lining up to let us poke around inside their heads."

"No kidding." Suliana pondered her father's statement.

"The older Raheeni are most susceptible. Hence the loss of our *Rahanarat*." Nupira winced. "We all have it in our blood. It just hasn't killed us yet."

Dralet watched his daughter's throat move and her unusual eyes fill with tears. He could almost feel the effort it took to bypass her emotions, to focus on the immediate need for information and action.

He had to fight against his pride. Later — if Raheen survived — perhaps he could tell her. But not right now.

"So." Suliana stood as if unable to keep still. She paced once more. "Raheen is infected. Or at least Raheeni blood is infected." She paused. "How? How is this…thing…this *agent*, spread?"

Dralet and Nupira turned to Parnulet. "That is the big question, and if I'm not mistaken our bad-tempered friend here may have the answer." Dralet raised an eyebrow.

Parnulet clicked keys, pushed various buttons and leaned back in his chair with a grimace. "I will. In just a moment or two. The last batch of data is being processed now."

Suliana nodded. "Another thing. You say that the elders are affected first, which makes sense. What about the average Raheeni? The younger ones?"

"More resistant. Younger organs, healthier tissue. More active circulation." Parnulet curled his lip. "Typical youthful physiology."

Nupira drew a breath. "We think...and this is only a theory right now...that it is possible the virus attacks an area of the brain that deals with logic. It weakens the links between it and the rest of the brain. Emotions are less controlled, less balanced."

"Passion becomes the overwhelming desire. The common sense that dictates the routine parts of life is diminished." Dralet simplified it.

"And the fields go untended while everybody fucks themselves to pieces and devours each other in *Arraho*." Suliana spoke as much to herself as anybody else.

"Exactly." Her father nodded.

"So why aren't they breeding?" Suliana's puzzled look flashed around at them. "With all the *Arraho*, why aren't there more children?"

"We're checking into that." Nupira shrugged. "There are only three of us, Suliana. We had to prioritize. First, find out if anything actually *was* killing us." She ticked off the points on her fingers. "Second, if something was killing us, what was it and how did it work?" She looked at Suliana. "And third, how do we stop it?"

Suliana stared back. "I'll give you a fourth. Where does it come from?"

The room fell silent. Dralet knew Suliana's question had pierced their deepest worries.

She closed her eyes for a moment. "It's alien, isn't it?"

Nupira gasped in surprise. "What makes you say that?"

"I'm not sure. Just that it seems logical. Why invade a planet and risk casualties if you can have an invisible virus do it for you?"

Suliana opened her eyes again, stunning Dralet. For a few moments they blazed with a strange blue and lavender light. "It's the perfect setup. The perfect plot, don't you see?" She almost stumbled over her words. "Raheen has shields, warning beacons, all sorts of mechanisms in place to detect incoming invasion fleets. And we've used them enough that they're probably pretty well known by now."

She turned to him. "So what is more logical than to invade with the *tiniest* of fleets? A microbe, a virus, something that will totally decimate the population of the planet you're after, and not result in one single casualty to you?"

A gleeful chuckle emanated from the other side of the console. "By the ray, that girl's got more brains than you have, old man." Parnulet grinned widely, showing his two remaining teeth with pride.

Dralet pinched the bridge of his nose. "It does make sense. Except for the fact that anything airborne would have affected everybody on Raheen, and probably a lot quicker than the time it's taken to kill off the *Rahanarat*. I know age is a factor, of course, but…"

"But it's not in the air." Parnulet almost leaped from his chair. "The air is clean." His jubilation was obvious, but failed to impress the others.

"One down. So it's not airborne. *How*, Parnulet? How is it spreading?" Nupira's voice shook.

"Great ray of light. Here I make a breakthrough that's stunning in its significance and all you want is more. Typical woman." Parnulet's gnarled fingers flew over the console.

He flicked a quick look at Suliana. "You'll appreciate that now we know what we're looking for, this process goes a whole lot quicker."

She nodded. "Makes sense."

"I do, at times." He stared back at the screen. "Come here."

Dralet eased himself into a chair, trying to deal with the notion that the future of his planet and all its inhabitants might rest on the slender shoulders of his daughter.

Or the woman who was, to all intents and purposes, his daughter. And yet…for a brief moment or two…he had looked into her eyes and seen a stranger.

Who was she now?

Suliana crossed the room to Parnulet's chair, then gasped as he raised her arm and gashed it with something sharp. The blood dripped freely down into a small dish...

* * * * *

While the Master and Mistress were engaged in their business, Suliana's *Tapa-hir* was regaining his strength.

Talot rested, eyes closed, aware that he had succeeded in his mission, and filled with triumph at the thought. Something else filled him as a hot tongue traced the length of his cock. Sleepily, he stirred, arousal sweeping through him. "Mmm. Mistress..."

A husky laugh greeted his words. "Why settle for her, when you can have the best?"

He opened his eyes and looked down his body to see Chanda lying comfortably between his legs. He blinked. Twice. "*Chanda?*"

"Hello, Talot." She cupped his balls, rolling them gently. "I wanted to see how you were doing."

His cock hardened visibly at her ministrations. *That's not all you're going to be seeing.*

"That's very...kind of you." He sucked in a breath as the tongue swiped once more, this time lingering around the growing ridge of arousal at the head of his cock.

"Are you feeling...stronger?"

Her hands fondled him, reaching beneath his balls and teasing the sensitive flesh she found there.

"Uhh...yes..."

"Good."

Talot jumped as two pinpricks galvanized his body. Chanda's fangs had nipped the soft skin of his inner hipbone.

"Like that?" She grinned at him as she licked the tiny injuries, white teeth a blinding contrast against the swollen redness of her lips. Her dark hair tumbled over his thighs, her bare body rubbed his legs...*what's not to like*?

"Mmm. I like your taste. Sweet. Hot." She flickered her eyelashes. "And powerful. You are *Tapa-hir*. I like *that.*"

Her mouth sucked him forcefully, teeth scraping the delicate skin along his cock. "Men with power are exciting. They arouse me."

She squeezed his balls—hard.

Talot moaned with pleasure. He felt the heady thrill of desire swell his veins, a need—a hunger.

"Oh yes, Talot. You need this, don't you?" Chanda pushed herself away from him, breasts hanging away from her body, her nipples hard and pointed. She leaned in, rubbing herself over his cock.

The taut nubs grazed him as her teeth sought the indentation of his navel and pierced him once more. "Ohhh...great ray...*yessss...*"

"Then let me play and give you what you need." She slithered across his body and reached for the ever-present straps that were a feature of beds all over the planet. Before Talot could utter a word, his wrists were secured above his head.

The bite of the cuffs into his flesh aroused him. Yes, Chanda was right. He *needed* this. He could never have his Mistress like this, if at all. Suliana was not for him.

But he could have others. Women like Chanda, who would be excited at the thought of sharing *Arraho* with the current *Tapa-hir*. It was one of the advantages, he supposed. To offset the knowledge that he could never have the woman he was pledged to serve.

Truly a double-edged sword.

Then the sharp fangs of the woman above him raked across one nipple, and he forgot all about Suliana, the *Tapa-hir* and everything but the exquisite pain.

"Oh my." A hot tongue licked across the bleeding flesh, healing it immediately. "You have beautiful nipples. They get so hard when I touch them." Chanda delicately gnawed on one, piercing it with her fang, tugging it away from his chest, and bringing sobs of lust to his throat.

She chuckled, a throaty sound that reverberated all the way to his balls. "Nice, Talot. Bet you wish you could return the favor, don't you?"

With a quick wriggle, she swung her full breasts over his face, just out of reach of his fully aroused fangs. "See my nipples, Talot? Want to suck them? Want to bite them? Pinch them until I beg you never to stop?"

He gulped and nodded as Chanda cupped her breasts and squeezed them together, mounding the flesh and making the taut nubs stand high on their peaks.

"Too bad."

Her pussy was pressed against his body, her heat searing him as her actions brought sharp pangs of need up behind Talot's eyes.

"Fuck me, you teasing bitch." He spat the words out, a gust of savagely erotic desire, fueled by the sheer unbridled sexuality of the woman sitting on his chest.

"All in good time."

Chanda slipped away from him, leaving Talot heaving deep, shuddering breaths, aching for more of what he knew she could give him.

She stood next to him, letting him see her hand as it slowly drifted down to the tuft of hair between her legs. Her long fingers stroked, her juices shining as she widened her stance and parted her pussy lips close to the pillow where he lay.

"Look, Talot. See how hot for you I am?" She smiled seductively. "And I can get hotter." A gleam entered her eyes. "I can get you hotter. Are you ready?"

Her scent filled his nostrils and his fangs emerged, harsh and hard against his mouth. His cock pulsed, moving slightly as it protruded rigidly away from his groin.

"I see you are. That's good." Chanda turned and reached into a bag behind her. "Let's see how far you and I can go."

She produced a long length of finely worked chain with a ring on the end. Working smoothly and efficiently, she snapped the ring around the base of Talot's cock. He winced as the cold metal tightened.

Experimentally, Chanda tugged on the other end.

Talot groaned aloud. "Great ray, woman. That is *sooo* good."

"It gets better." Chanda reached behind her once more and two nipple clamps appeared in her hand. She leaned over and snapped them in place. On Talot.

His breath left his lungs at the sharp pain. And returned in a rush as Chanda threaded the chain through the two loops, binding his cock to his nipples. Each pulse, each thud of his heart echoed along the length of his erection, through the ring and the chain and tugged on his nipples.

It was exquisite agony.

"Now we ride, my sweet. Ride the road to ecstasy." Chanda straddled Talot, brushing his cock and moving it with her pussy. Each touch, each thrust coinciding with a bolt of sheer electricity along Talot's nerve endings.

His balls were rock-hard, drawn up tight beneath the restrained arousal. As Chanda moved, Talot choked out his pleasure and his pain, his fangs starting to leak juices as his need to feed and take *Arraho* grew exponentially with Chanda's sexual torture.

It got even more intense when Chanda finally parted her pussy lips once more. "See, Talot? Watch." She yanked on the chain to get his attention. He figured his scream ought to tell her she had it.

Swollen flesh parted, glistening folds shining between her fingers. Her pearly clit was protruding hungrily, as were her fangs. "Are you ready for me?"

"Yes." Talot fought for command of his voice. But it was a near thing. Two more heartbeats and he would explode.

She hovered over him, brushing the wetness of her cunt against the oozing slit of his cock, her movements translating into savage tugs on his inflamed and sensitive nipples.

He hungered. "*Arraho*, Chanda. I want your *Arraho*." He stared at her, furious, aroused, desperate in so many ways he could barely form the words.

Their gazes met and locked, purple flames entwining, bodies straining, and fangs glistening.

Chanda lowered her eyelids. With a little exclamation of pleasure, she lowered herself onto his cock. "Yes, *Tapa-hir*. As you command."

Her scalding cunt enveloped him, and as she began to move the chain pulled and loosened, and his cock engorged with blood trapped by the ring.

She drove him to his limits and past them, and when the red haze of his blood misted his vision, he screamed for her.

"Now, Chanda. Give me your *Arraho. Now*."

Talot poured every ounce of command he possessed into his voice, and Chanda responded. She thrust her hips down onto him and leaned forward, pressing her wrist to his mouth. "Take it, Talot. Take *Arraho*."

As she spoke the words, Talot's fangs ripped into her flesh. Her blood, darkly maroon and hot, flowed copiously into his mouth. He drank thirstily, her heat fueling his own orgasm and driving him over the brink.

Pulse after pulse, wave after wave, the climax roared through him, and Chanda's fangs sank into his breast beneath the nipple clamp. She sucked him with her mouth and her cunt, spasming around him as he exploded inside her.

She moaned, her fangs buried deep, tearing into his flesh and feasting on his passion and desire.

They hung, trembling, riding out the aftershocks, thirsting for more, but too sated to pursue it.

Finally, Talot released her, licking the scars his feeding had left. They disappeared, leaving her skin unblemished.

He felt…relaxed. Tired but relaxed.

Chanda licked him in her turn and released his restraints. "That was truly incredible, Talot."

She curled up on his chest and ran a fingertip over his pink nipple. "Thank you, *my Tapa-hir.*"

Chapter Eight

Suliana was breathless by the time she arrived at Noul Keirat's door. Her trip to the *Rahanarat* had taken most of the day, far longer than she'd anticipated, and the news she had to impart wouldn't wait a minute more.

Time is of the essence. The phrase flashed through her brain. *Damn straight.*

She flung the door wide to see Keirat raise a glass to his lips. "*Stop!*"

Her shriek startled Keirat and he jumped, slurping the liquid over himself. "Oh for…" He brushed crossly at his robe. "You could give me some warning before erupting in here like that."

"Sorry." She waved it aside. "What's in that?" She stared at his goblet.

He tilted his head at her and frowned. "Wine. Why?"

She breathed out in relief. "Because the *water's contaminated*, that's why."

Keirat rocked back on his heels, staring at her. "*What?*"

Suliana sank into a chair and struggled to calm the furious thundering of her heart. "I've been with the *Rahanarat* all day. They have found out so much…explained so much…and I…" Tears filled her eyes. "My father is one of the last ones."

Keirat crossed to the chair and knelt beside it. "I know, Suli. It is an honor. Why do you cry?"

"I don't want him to die too." She wailed out her concern, her pain, to the one man she could trust.

And he took her in his arms. "We will all die eventually. It is the way of things."

"But not like *this*." She pulled away a little, resting her hands on his chest. "I was serious, Keirat. The water has been contaminated. Poisoned with a bacteria. Parnulet, Nupira, my father…they've been working on it for so long. They've just put it all together."

Keirat moved, pulling his chair from behind his desk and tugging it next to hers. "Tell me."

Suli fought for control. "Okay. Here's the thing. The last invasion was unsuccessful. But they believe that somehow, one of the invaders got through, survived perhaps, and planted a contaminant in the water supply. It's a bacteria that attacks the brain cells in a certain way, and it's turning the Raheeni into sex-crazed idiots. It destroys the area of the brain that handles logic—"

She made a helpless gesture with her hand. "I'm a bit vague on the details of this stuff. It's really technical."

Keirat simply nodded. "Go on."

"Well, after they'd ruled out an airborne threat, they started checking other possible contamination sources. And the water was the second place they looked." She pursed her lips. "It was there, Keirat. In the water. Plain as day when they knew what to look for. Raheen wells are poisoned."

Keirat ran a hand over his face. "You're serious, aren't you?"

"You betcha. I couldn't be *more* serious. Raheen is being invaded, right this minute, only from within, not from the skies."

Keirat blinked at the odd expression, but couldn't allow himself to be distracted from the main point of discussion. "So why aren't we all dead? We all drink water, right?"

"It's slow-acting. Vicious little bugger. Takes its time to infect and destroy. The older ones go first, since they drink more water and have less resistance."

"Hence the deaths of the *Rahanarat*?" Keirat raised an eyebrow.

"You got it. And also hence the great urge to head out for *Arraho* instead of the fields." She sighed. "We thought it was simply our nature. It's not. It's a little death for all of us."

He frowned. "Suli, this sounds really farfetched."

"Oh, I know. Believe me, I know. I couldn't have written a better plot for a science fiction story if my life depended on it." She frowned in her turn. "Uhh…"

She froze for a moment as images of books and words flashed across her neural pathways. They were alien, but familiar — a part of her mind that shared her dreams, perhaps, or some memory from her past. It was too ingrained to be anything other than her own thoughts, although consciously she'd have had a hard time identifying any of the images. She shook her head. Time for introspection later — *after* the crisis was solved. "But I saw it, on the console, under the microscope. It's there, Keirat. In the wells. And of course with the drought, the well water has been used continually. It's not been refreshed by rainwater or diluted in any way."

Keirat raised an eyebrow. "So why aren't I dead? Or some sex-crazed maniac?"

Suliana stared at him.

He cleared his throat. "Well, all right. When it comes to *you* I'm a sex-crazed maniac. But you know what I mean."

She squelched down the pang of lust his words had aroused. She had to finish this, to tell him what needed to be done. "You drink wine. Mostly wine, yes?"

He nodded.

"And have you been feeling perfectly well lately?"

"Yes."

"Honestly?" She pursued it. "No aches or pains?"

Involuntarily, his hand went to the back of his neck, the spot he caught himself massaging on a pretty regular basis.

"I knew it." She sat back. "Headache, right?"

He glared at her. "Now and again."

"It's begun. You are not as seriously affected as those who drink more water. And the younger and stronger you are, the longer it takes to attack." She shook her head. "It's insidious, Keirat. Clever, extremely clever, and a product of a technology that is way beyond ours."

He blew a breath out between his lips. "Suli, are you sure? These aren't the ramblings of a few old people with nothing better to do with their lives?"

She drew herself up straight in her chair. "No, Keirat. This is the truth. I have seen it with my own eyes. I'm not a scientist but the data was clear. And, for your information, my father has a *lot* better things to do with his life than devote it to isolating some stupid invading *bug*…"

* * * * *

Keirat observed his mate's flashing eyes and twitching jaw and made a note to himself to watch what he said about her father in future.

Then he turned his mind to what she'd told him. "So if it's in the water…"

"It's in everything that uses the water." Suliana finished his sentence. "It's in the food we eat, the liquids we make from the fruits…" She nodded at his goblet. "It's even in the wine, although since grapes grow more slowly there's probably not as concentrated an amount."

The full impact of the situation began to dawn on Keirat. His planet, his *people*, were being systematically poisoned by an alien plague. He stood and walked to the window, trying to get his head around the concept.

"Fuck."

Suliana nodded. "Yeah. I pretty much said the same thing." She bit her lip. "Especially when…"

"When what?"

"When it was suggested that the agent is continually being introduced into the water. That there may be an alien still here, on Raheen."

Keirat opened his mouth, but Suliana's hand stopped him. "I know. There are no aliens. Which leads us to only one conclusion. The invader has become one of us. A Raheeni. Either by taking over a body, or adapting their own. Nobody knows." She snorted. "Nupira assures me the technological level of development that made this virus possible means these aliens are quite capable of either scenario."

"We have a saboteur." He spoke slowly, trying to comprehend the disaster that could befall them. No, *was* befalling them.

"Possibly. I suppose we'll find out if and when we can clear the water supply. If it becomes re-contaminated, then yes. We have a saboteur."

Keirat sucked in air. *Great ray of light.* How had things gone so wrong? And on his watch, too. He stretched his neck, struggling for control. "So now we know."

"Er…Keirat? There's more."

He set his shoulders, squaring them in readiness. "Tell me. Tell me the whole of it."

"They ran my blood through their analyzers. I'm immune."

Her voice was calm, but he could detect the undercurrent of excitement that ran beneath. "I have no idea why. Perhaps something I brought with me when I returned. Maybe some small portion of my physiology was affected by the host for all those cycles. I'm not sure and neither are the *Rahanarat*." She paused. "But do you know what that means?"

"It means *you* will live. Here, on a planet where people are dying around you." He clenched his teeth. "Your mate included."

Suliana's face dropped. "Oh no, *noooo*." She rushed from her chair to hug him tight. "It means that when we share *Arraho*, you will share my immunity. You will feed from me, Keirat. You will take whatever it is that makes me immune into you."

He blinked. "And it won't kill me?"

"Of course not. Parnulet ran a mixture of my blood with theirs. Already the symptoms are lessening."

"That's all well and good, but you can't feed the entire damned planet." Keirat hissed his frustration. "Am I supposed to choose who you will feed? Pick those who will live and those who die?"

Suliana gritted her teeth. "Stop being so fucking melodramatic and listen to me." She shook him, hands fisted in his robe. "The *Rahanarat* have bought *time* for themselves with my blood. Time to develop a filter for the water system at the least, or if we're *really* lucky, something that will kill the poison stone dead." Her grip turned gentle. "We must buy *you* time, Keirat. With my blood in you, you will be able to maintain control. You know what is happening to our people. It will not happen to you, and you'll be the ruler you must be at this time. Strong, calm, and able to quell the fears that will spread like wildfire if — *when* — this news gets out."

Her eyes blazed, strange colors blending around the dark centers, her passion and her feelings written clearly across her face. "Keirat, we *must* share *Arraho. Now.*"

He nearly laughed. Would have, if the situation hadn't been so serious. He'd been preparing himself to make the same demand and she'd beaten him to it. But her reasons were so much larger than his.

Or were they? Keirat's thoughts whirled. "Suli, I have news for you too."

She stared at him. "Oh?"

"Chanda is going to answer your challenge herself. I think she means to kill you." He pulled her close and held her, relishing in the way she nestled so readily against him. "You are still not at your full strength. You need mine. I was drinking that wine to give me enough courage to ask you something. To share *Arraho* with me. *Now.*"

She lifted her head and stared at him, following it with her hand. Softly, her fingertips brushed his cheek, his brow and down the length of his nose, ending at his lips.

He couldn't help himself. He kissed them. There was something about her, his chosen mate, that touched him in so many ways. He suddenly realized that he loved her. With his soul. And it was completely unexpected.

Raheeni were not known for their loving, only their passion. He'd felt that passion for Suliana in the Glade, but hadn't realized that when she returned he'd feel this odd melting sensation deep inside him. A warmth that had nothing to do with sex and everything to do with her.

He was, to put it bluntly, screwed up. And more than a little embarrassed by the whole thing. The Suliana he'd chosen had been a Raheeni woman he knew would be his mate. The Suliana who had awoken in his arms was so much more.

As a slow smile curved her lips, his heart stirred along with his loins. Theirs would indeed be a magnificent *Arraho*. But Keirat knew for certain it would be more than just an orgasm and a feeding. This time it would be an exchange of hearts.

"Keirat..." Her gaze roamed his face. "Keirat."

"What?" His arms refused to release her.

"I want you." She licked her lips. A tiny movement but one that lit a fire inside him. "I want you *now.*"

"As you wish."

The Master surrendered.

* * * * *

What Adella thought as she hurriedly responded to the summons from her Mistress, Suliana had no idea.

What she thought when both Master and Mistress announced they were about to share *Arraho*—*now*—was evident.

"*What*? You *can't*."

"We can, and we must." Keirat's voice was uncompromising.

"He's right, Adella. It's an absolute necessity. The future of Raheen depends on it." Suliana added her might.

Adella's eyes narrowed. "You two are so hungry for each other, you're willing to throw away centuries of tradition…just to *fuck*?" She was clearly outraged.

"Adella." Suliana took the woman's hands and covered them with both of hers. "Of course we're hungry for each other. We're mated. Master and Mistress. But with those titles comes a responsibility to our world. This *Arraho* is completely and absolutely imperative for *Raheen*, not just us."

"She's right."

Adella jumped at the voice behind her. It was Talot. "She is correct, Mother." He held a tray with two glasses on it. "They must share *Arraho*."

Suliana risked a quick glance at Keirat. His face was expressionless as he spoke to Talot. "I'm glad you concur, *Tapa-hir*."

"Well, I'm not." Adella turned to her son. "You support this madness?"

His face was sober. "Yes, I do."

"Why? You, of all people? You're *Tapa-hir*. You know the traditions of Raheen. You're supposed to be helping our Mistress, our people, not violating everything we hold sacred."

Talot looked embarrassed. "I concur with the Master and Mistress for a very good reason, Mother."

"It had better be more than just *good*, my son."

Keirat fidgeted. Suliana choked back a chuckle. This was serious stuff, but after all the talking would come the fucking. Her mate obviously had his mind on the end product rather than the means it took to get there.

"Chanda was in my room earlier." Talot stared at nothing in particular.

"Oh?" Keirat was still now.

"She…I…well, we…"

Suliana spared him. "We understand. Go on."

He shot her a look of gratitude. "Yes, well…something she said, and the way she said it, made me uncomfortable. I realized after she'd left that it could easily imply harm to you, Mistress." He raised troubled eyes to Suliana. "I will not allow that to happen."

Keirat nodded. "It is decided. And, for what it's worth, Talot, I agree. Chanda does mean harm to Suli. We must protect her at all costs." He turned slightly. "Adella?"

The older woman sighed. "I don't like this. I don't like it at all." She stared at Keirat and then at Suliana. "But these are troubled times. Desperate times. Perhaps…perhaps a break from the past is what is needed."

"Thank you, Adella." Suliana heaved a breath of relief. "You will help me prepare?"

"Yes." Adella's face looked worried, but she nodded. "I will do all that is necessary."

"Thank you." Her words came from the bottom of Suliana's heart. Adella would never know just how desperate matters were. Not right at this moment, anyway.

Keirat looked at Talot. "What did Chanda say?"

Talot shifted uncomfortably. "Well, it was in the aftermath of…er…"

"*What did she say?*" There was no mistaking the tone of command.

"She called me *her Tapa-hir*." He blushed and looked at Suliana. "Not *yours*."

Chapter Nine

There was a hushed bustle in the quarters of the Master and Mistress. Adella whisked Suliana off to the bath, while Talot made the room ready for their *Arraho.*

"Ordinarily, you would be going to the Glade, Suliana." Adella's voice still held tinges of rebuke as she stripped Suliana's robe from her.

"I know. But to be honest, I'd rather have it this way." Suliana stepped into the scented bathwater. "Something about fucking one's brains out in public doesn't really appeal to me. Not when it's this important, anyway."

Adella shook her head and pinned Suliana's hair out of the way. "I don't understand any of this, I really don't."

"You're better off that way." Suliana dipped her shoulders beneath the water, wondering if it, too, was contaminated. Hell, she wasn't *drinking* the damn stuff. It had to be ingested, right? And anyway, she was immune.

It didn't help the bath experience though, that was for sure. She banished the thought and another popped into its place. "Adella, do you read much?"

Adella paused in her bathing chores. "Pardon?"

"Read. You know, books. Novels."

"Er…" Adella reached for the soap, a frown crossing her face. "That's for scholars. Or those with more time than I. Besides, I wouldn't understand all that technical stuff, anyway." She lathered Suliana's shoulders. "What's a novel?"

"Oh *maaaan*…" Suliana grinned. "It's a story. An invented tale about people. An adventure, a love story, whatever…sometimes it has lots of sex in it."

Adella snorted. "Right. We're too busy *doing* it to read about it. I can't see the point."

"Really."

"Besides, why on earth would we want to read an invented story about invented people? It doesn't make sense, Suliana. I doubt there'd be much interest, if you'll forgive my saying so. Best leave the reading to the scholars and the *Rahanarat*."

"Hmm." Suliana closed her eyes and enjoyed the luxury of having someone else wash her back. "We'll see…"

"Now." Adella rinsed off the lather. "I have your robe ready."

She held out a large towel and Suliana stepped out of the bath. "Thank you, *Matriha*."

"And as *Matriha*, I must ask if you are willing and ready to take *Arraho* with your Master?"

A slow heat ignited in Suliana's body. "Oh *yeah*."

In spite of herself, Adella grinned. "That's good."

She straightened and helped Suliana into the deepest purple robe, fastening the two small buttons at the waist. They were all that held it together. *Talk about easy access.* Suliana glanced down at the opening that clearly revealed most of her breasts and just about all of her pussy if she so much as breathed.

Would Keirat like it?

Adella answered her unasked question. "You are beautiful, Mistress Suliana. A fitting mate for the Master."

Suliana hugged her. "Thank you, *Matriha*." She swallowed. "Let's go. I've got a fucking to attend."

* * * * *

Keirat was ready. As ready as he'd ever be. Talot had placed the ceremonial wine near the bed and helped arrange the toys needed.

There had been whips to sort through, the bar needed double checking to make sure it was secure above the mattress...what seemed like a thousand and one small details to a man about to mate with his woman.

Finally, he dismissed Talot with a nod of thanks, unable to find appropriate words. Talot didn't seem to mind. He smiled and left.

For a moment, the room was empty, holding its breath—like Keirat. Waiting for *her*. Like Keirat.

And then she was there.

He sensed her presence moments before she spoke, a faint fragrance of flowers and Suliana. His cock leaped between his thighs and his balls tingled.

"I am here, Master."

Her head was bent, eyes lowered correctly.

"I offer you my submission. My surrender. My *Arraho* is yours to do with as you will."

The words were traditional, but the look she flashed him from beneath her lashes was anything *but*. Impish, mischievous and *hot*, her eyes blazed. She wanted him as much, if not more, than he wanted her.

He swallowed. "I accept your *Arraho*. And in so doing I accept you as my Mistress."

How he ground out the response, he had no idea, since his teeth were clenched hard, fighting the desire this woman aroused in him. But fight it, he would. He *must*. This would be a joining for the record books if he had anything to say about it.

"Remove your robe." Keirat leaned back against an ornately carved wooden chest. He was already naked, his cock standing proudly erect. Suliana was, for this moment, his submissive mate. And yet he wondered who would actually submit to whom.

She obeyed, quickly slipping the two buttons free and allowing the purple stuff to slide to the floor.

Great ray of light, she was beautiful. Her silver curls brushed the upper swells of her breasts, and the shining stuff gleamed on the mound between her legs. A thin strip, no more, but enough to point the way to where he wanted to be.

As if he needed guidance.

Keirat shook off the spell her naked body had cast upon him. "On the bed."

Suliana moved, clambering onto the high mattress.

"Stand."

She blinked, then followed his instructions, swaying a little at her uncertain footing.

Keirat followed her, biting back his arousal as her naked body brushed his. His fangs ached, but had yet to emerge. How he held them back, he had no idea.

"Extend your arms out." He reached for the bar and pulled it down on its chain until it rested across her shoulders. With two swift moves, he cuffed her wrists to each end of the bar. She was held there, at his mercy.

He licked his lips. Oh yes. *There* were his fangs. To help his control, he put some distance between their naked bodies, climbing off the bed to stand next to it.

"Kneel."

She tugged on the bar, finding the chain flexible enough to allow her to kneel on the bed.

And there she was. His mate. A silver-haired beauty, naked, restrained, and ready for his pleasure. He allowed himself a moment to appreciate the picture she made, thighs splayed wide as she balanced herself, her head respectfully lowered, her ass a work of art, curved and white, resting just above her heels.

His palm itched.

Without further ado, Keirat brought his arm down, smacking the white buttock hard.

She swayed forward, the chain locking into place as she moved.

Again, he slapped her, the sound of flesh meeting flesh filling the silent room. Her cheek was reddening, but the color wasn't restricted to her ass. A flood of arousal was beginning, spreading over her limbs.

Keirat leaned over and allowed himself a taste of the pleasures to come.

He sank his fangs into her buttock—and drank.

* * * * *

With the first smack on her backside, Suliana heated to boiling point. This was what she'd wanted, craved, for so long. The second slap sent the blood pounding through her, and when his teeth pierced her, she moaned.

So good. So *very* good. The stinging pain shot through her, arousing her.

His tongue swiped the punctures, healing them, and she waited. What would be next? Did she care? Anything he did, wanted, needed…it was his. *She* was his. Stretched as she was, her breasts thrust forward, their peaks hard already.

Great ray, she was excited. Tremors of desire crept delicately over her skin, and when his hand landed hard on her other buttock, she sobbed out her delight. "Yessss…"

No bite followed, though. This time a whistling sound made her blink and quickly the sting of a lash landed, catching her across both cheeks. "Mmmm." She moaned once more, loving the pain. "More."

It was a whisper, but he heard her. And he gave her what she needed.

More.

Sharp, quick slashes, followed by longer, harder blows, the tip of the lash licking at her flesh just seconds before his tongue lapped her blood and healed the scars. Her back, her buttocks—

eventually he moved around to find her breasts, swollen and heated and ready.

His first lash flicked across a nipple, opening a tiny wound. He was fucking *good* with that whip. She drank the sharp agony thirstily, feeling it shimmer through her body to her clit.

His head quickly followed, tongue hungrily feeding, suckling, teasing the pain away.

Suliana moaned aloud, letting her head loll back and her eyes drift shut. She was alive to his every move, his every punishment, desiring it, needing it—hungering for the passion released by this exquisite pain.

Her fangs were already extended, oozing their own healing fluids. She could sense the moisture between her thighs, too, and there was nothing oozing about the flood of arousal soaking her.

The bed dipped as Keirat's weight pushed it down, and she opened her eyes to see him climb up in front of her.

He grasped his cock in one hand and her hair in the other. "Your mouth. On me. Now."

His voice was harsh, but his fingers were gentle as he pushed the head of his cock past her fangs and into her mouth. She took him willingly, wanting him, wanting *this*…

It had been denied her for too long. Too many nights in the Glade when she'd have killed to get a chance to suck him. Well, now she could and it was time to make up for missed opportunities.

Suliana licked him, tongue alive to his taste, the feel of his velvet hardness at the back of her throat. She let her fangs graze him as he pulled out, loving the little tremor that shook him as he thrust in again.

He was spicy and sweet and tangy—everything she'd wanted and more. She learned the ridges and dips of his cock with her tongue, and learned what he liked, although there wasn't much he didn't like.

She ached to bury her fingernails in his buttocks, carve the solid flesh and pull him closer, but she was restrained. At his mercy. She had to accept what he gave her. For now, anyway.

Slick with her saliva, his cock plunged again and again into her mouth, plundering her, filling her with his taste, his scent, the heat of his body burning her face as he thrust hard, going deeper than she'd imagined possible.

Her throat opened for him as her cunt ached for him. Suliana wanted to suck him dry, rip into the sac that swung beneath his cock, feed from him, take him so far inside her that she would explode from it.

She hungered.

And he knew.

He groaned as he pulled free of her mouth. "Enough."

No. No. Never enough. The words screamed through Suliana's brain, but at that moment he dropped to his knees in front of her and sank a fang into her nipple.

She screamed, throat still longing for his cock. The pain was torture, magnificent wonderful torture, and when he pinched the other nipple with his hand, she cried out once more. "*Yes, Master. Oh yes…*"

He tugged on her breasts, pulling them taut, playing with them, only to release them, heal the wound and reverse positions. Now the other breast was pierced and as he drank, sparks of desire shot through Suliana, a painful pleasure that galvanized every nerve ending, shook her body and ended in her cunt.

She choked back her cries of ecstasy, knowing that each time she released them he would stop, move to another place, and begin the punishment all over again. She wasn't sure if she could stand it should he cease his torture.

But Keirat didn't need her cries for guidance. He seemed to sense her responses, flawlessly timing his punishment with her arousal. She was burning hot, her body suffused with the heat of desire. The heat of passion, the heat of pain, the heat of a sensual agony that racked her.

He stood and pulled hard on the chain, jerking the bar upwards and bringing Suliana to her feet.

He knelt before her, and she looked down, past the blood streaking her, past the ruby red nipples, to his head, hair gleaming purple-black against her white skin.

His breath seared her pussy as his fingers pulled the swollen folds apart. Slowly, carefully, with infinite patience, Keirat sank his fang into her clit.

And Suliana cried out, a great sound that rattled her soul.

* * * * *

Keirat sucked her. Fed on her. Took her blood with his fangs and her moisture with his tongue. The blend of her tastes drove him crazy, filling him with a desire for her that threatened to detonate his cock.

He kept a fang securely through the small pearl of flesh, knowing the magnificent agony it would bring her. Then he let his tongue play, pushing between her pussy lips, toying with the opening to her cunt, lapping her juices and returning once more to tease that quivering clit.

He could feel her struggle to remain still, her thighs twitching as he gripped them hard enough to leave marks. She wanted to move, and the denial made the wanting all the sweeter.

Her blood was fire in his mouth, her scent fuel for his own arousal. Her cries were echoed by the clenching of his balls, and he was higher than he'd ever been in his life. If her nipples had been delicious, her cunt was the finest wine, and he snarled as he buried his face in her.

Great ray, he could devour this woman and still not get enough.

"*Keirat...*" Her mewling sob speared him, sending a shudder of lust through his groin to his cock. He pulled on her thighs, parting her legs even wider, knowing her wrists would be chafing now as they took more of her weight.

She could go higher.

He slid his fang free, licking and suckling her clit whole, and enjoying her sobs of delight. He set his own needs aside, even though the merest touch of air on his cock was a torture all its own.

Her pussy cried for him, juices pouring freely from her, soaking his face and his hands as he spread her as wide as he could. More, always more. Would there ever be enough with his mate? Keirat doubted they'd ever find out.

He bent to her once more, this time letting his fangs knife down the soft flesh on either side of her clit. Thin red lines followed, dripping blood that Keirat feasted on, drank thirstily, and healed. Only to repeat the process all over again.

The heat between them was intense, Suliana's body fiery with her arousal, and Keirat's blood an inferno of desire. He thrust three fingers deep into her cunt as he slashed her pussy once more, and she cried out in an agony of pleasure.

Yet again he fed and feasted on the very essence of her, this time feeling her cunt as it shook around his intrusive fingers. Hot, wet, slippery, it was nearing readiness for his possession, even as her blood thickened in her veins, flowing more slowly now as desire peaked within her body.

They were close. So close.

Keirat tore his mouth from her, fighting to control the red flames of lust that began to blur his vision.

He rose before her, ripping his fangs up the length of her body, from pussy to breasts. Red scars opened for him, and his tongue traced them, sealing them as he sipped from them, hot tears of passion dripping from her own fangs to mingle with his.

Finally they stood, face to face, and Keirat stared into her eyes.

They were unfocused, and she blinked as she struggled to maintain her control. Bright purple lights flickered behind the blue-lavender irises, her pupils dilated, her lids heavy.

"Keirat..." She struggled with the words. "I surrender *Arraho*."

A whisper, no more, but one that pierced Keirat to his soul.

He ripped the chains from her wrists, pushed the bar aside and pulled her back down to her knees. Her hands fell on his shoulders as she steadied herself.

He lifted her, arranged her legs around his hips and kept her poised above his cock. "I accept your surrender, Suliana." He had to say the words somehow, to complete this ritual, but it was harder than he'd ever imagined. The buzz of lust in his ears, the ache of his building orgasm in his balls, and the fire of passion Suliana had aroused in him — it was almost too much to bear.

One hand slid around her hips to her back, his fingers finding her cleft, seeking, searching for that little muscular ring that had welcomed his cock.

She shivered as he found it.

"I accept your *Arraho*. And I offer mine in return."

With a shudder, Keirat lifted Suliana higher then dropped her as his cock thrust upwards. She came onto his body, impaled by his hardness, smashed up against his chest and with his finger buried in her ass.

Her lips curled back as the first shudders of her orgasm ran through her, and Keirat felt his own fangs vibrate in response.

The tingling in his balls grew, expanded, turned into a flood of prickling pain and forced his mouth open on a snarl of passion.

Her cunt quivered around him, her ass muscles began to shake, and she worked her throat as it began.

"Keirat...*Master*...*Arraho*..." She screamed, her eyes blind as her body trembled in his grasp.

"Suliana...*Mistress*...*Arraho*..." Keirat screamed in his turn, his cock pulsing and throbbing now as his semen filled it, pressure building beyond his limits to control.

With one move, they lowered their heads and tore into each other.

The Master and the Mistress fed their *Arraho*. Surrender, submission and satisfaction.

The cycle was finally complete. They were one.

Chapter Ten

With the first slash of her fangs into Keirat, Suliana's world exploded. With the gush of his blood into her mouth and down her throat, her orgasm shattered her and her mind opened, taking her into a new realm of sensation.

Every single second seemed an eternity, one in which she could fathom the mysteries of the universe, if not creation itself.

Lights crackled in her optic nerves, matching the crackle and spark that fizzed along the inside of her cunt. Keirat's cock ravaged her, pounding against her, sending her into a frenzy of orgasmic pleasure that only whirled her further into the void.

She hung on to his chest by her teeth, sucking, drinking, swallowing his life fluid, even as he drank from her. Dizzy and reeling from the overload of sensation, Suliana let go, following where her body led.

It took her to a place where Keirat's thoughts were her thoughts, where Keirat's world became her world, and where she and Keirat were no longer two people but one. One giant climax, one set of rippling muscles. One cock embedded in one cunt, separate no more.

She felt what he felt. The twitches as his balls continued to flood her. The milking caresses of her inner walls as they translated into cramping delights against her clit. She tasted herself in his mouth as he would taste himself in hers.

Their minds blended as their bodies merged. Their souls, separated by time and space, interlocked into a new and perfect form, linked forever by the exchange of blood between them at this moment of orgasm.

And the moment went on — and on.

Each drop of the other's blood fired up their climax once more. Suliana swallowed Keirat's blood, only to feel her pussy clench, her clit boil against him, and the spasms continue unabated.

He sucked from her and his cock throbbed, continually spurting, filling her, overflowing her, soaking them both with his come. And along with the orgasm came the mental images, the influx of everything that was Noul Keirat. Flooding her brain as fully as his cock flooded her cunt.

She saw his youth, his strength, the challenges he'd survived to become what he was—her Master and her mate. And she saw Raheen, as he'd seen it. A planet troubled by drought, fraught with political intrigue, and as she saw this, she felt his frustration, his agony at his helplessness.

She didn't know she could love him any more than she did already, but this particular sensation reached far beyond any emotion she'd yet experienced. Her heart twisted as she experienced his pain.

This was not the pain of pleasure, or the pain of injury. This was the pain of failure, of his inabilities to make things right for his people. His heart was laid bare before her mind's eye, and even as she continued to orgasm, Suliana shared that particular ache and longed to ease it.

The best she could do was to feed him, nourish him and give him everything she had—everything she was.

* * * * *

For his part, Keirat fed from Suliana with the expectations of sharing an orgasm like no other. And this was happening. His cock seemed unbounded by physical limits, his balls continually refilling, emptying themselves over and over into his mate.

But then he began to share in *her*, in her essence, her spirit and her brain. He shared her orgasm, marveling at the sensation of a clit, of how it responded to his ravaging thrusts, of how it felt to have a cunt spasming inside one's body and breasts that swelled and heated to the point of exquisite rapture.

And he saw her heart.

He saw strange places, blue skies, buildings that were unfamiliar and faces of people he did not know. He saw words, blinking on a datascreen, flying from hands he knew were his but did not recognize. There was no rationality, no point of reference for him, he simply flew down the path of her consciousness, absorbing it, learning from it, and sensing the strength, the will and the compassion of the woman he was devouring.

He sensed her enormous curiosity, her thirst for knowledge and the desire for him and his world that had pulled her free of her shell and thrust her into Suliana, to become a part of her forever. And to become a part of him.

He understood now some of what made Suliana unique. And he loved her more for it. He loved the woman she had become. He loved the body that he was connected to by his fangs and his cock, and he loved the soul that his feeding had touched.

The heat of her filled his mouth and his throat as he drank, and the heat of her surrounded his cock as he spewed everything he had, everything he was, into her depths.

This was Arraho. A true *Arraho*, where not just bodies blended, but minds and souls as well. Tears leaked from his eyes, streaking his face and sliding unnoticed into the blood that poured into his mouth.

Heat flooded him, Suliana filled him — he was complete. He was whole. The parts of him that had ached and lain empty were now full, packed with thoughts, ideas and emotions she'd given him.

And he was dying from the pleasure of it.

He had to pull away. They both had to pull away. But it was the hardest thing he'd ever done.

Keirat knew it was up to him. Suliana didn't have the strength to separate herself from this *Arraho*. She was as seduced as he was, as thirsty as he was, and more than willing to continue the feeding as they fucked.

But the little lights dancing at the sides of his vision warned him that it was time to stop, before they literally killed each other.

Grabbing the little strength he had left, Keirat pulled his fangs free of Suliana's flesh, laving the harsh wounds, healing them, sealing them and breaking the connection between them.

He heard her cry out, a sharp sound of loss and emptiness. He recognized it. He felt the same way.

And yet he was not empty. Not now.

Carefully he ploughed his fingers through her hair and eased her head from his body. Instinctively her tongue sought the wound she had made and in her turn she healed her lover's injuries.

The scars faded, the skin became flawless, and they hung there for a moment, separate but joined, breathless, spent, but alive in a new and astonishingly vibrant way.

Then they surrendered and tumbled into a heap on the bed.

A great lethargy swamped Keirat. His body ached and his mind was swollen with the experience, unable to cope.

He hugged Suliana close and dragged a cover awkwardly over their legs. His eyes closed and he gave up the struggle to stay awake.

It was time for them both to sleep.

* * * * *

And sleep they did. Talot tapped several times on their door the following morning, without eliciting a response. Finally, he peered inside, to see a tangle of limbs smothered by the covers, snuffling and snoring contentedly.

Talot smiled. The *Arraho* had obviously been a good one. He silently entered, and began straightening up, picking the lash

182

off the chair where it had been flung, shaking out and folding his Mistress's robe, and generally being useful.

He glanced at the tray — and was hit with a sudden terrible thought. He had brought them the wine. As *Tapa-hir*, he held the ceremonial stone containers in his room. And *Chanda* had been in his room.

He bit his lip as he tried to remember if she'd slept first, or if he'd fallen asleep before she had. If she'd had the time or the opportunity to do something to that wine, knowing full well who would be the only people drinking it.

He had to find out.

With a shaking hand he reached for the smaller goblet, the one designated for the Mistress. He raised it to his nose. It smelled right. He raised it to his lips.

"Talot?" Suliana's sleepy voice came from the bed. "What are you doing?" She yawned and stretched. "What time is it?"

Talot jumped and put the wine down. "Er...it is morning, Mistress."

Keirat's tousled head emerged from beneath the pillows. "Morning? *Already*?"

Talot stared as the Master opened his eyes. "*Master*."

Keirat blinked and yawned in his turn. "What?"

"Your eyes." Talot stuttered to a halt. "They...they're..."

Suliana turned to look at Keirat. Keirat blinked at her. "They look fine to me, Talot. What are you talking about?"

Talot stared once more at the Master. Rich purple eyes looked back, showing none of the flashes of strange colors Talot could've sworn he saw just seconds ago. He shook his head. "Never mind."

Keirat rolled his neck, cracking bones and making Suliana wince. "Ouch."

Talot grinned, then turned somber as he remembered what he'd been doing. "Uh, Master? Mistress? Did you drink any of the wine?"

"There wasn't really time for wine, Talot." Suliana raised one eyebrow as she glanced at Keirat. A heated look passed between them and Talot blushed.

"Why?" Keirat lay back on the pillows, hands behind his head.

"I had a horrid thought. What with Chanda being in my room, and the wine being kept in there…I sort of put the puzzle pieces together and came up with a nasty picture." He shrugged. "But I'm sure I must be wrong."

Suliana thought for a moment. "Never hurts to be on the safe side, Talot. You did the right thing mentioning it."

"Thank you, Mistress. Shall I run your bath?"

A huge smile greeted his words. *I'm guessing that's a yes.* "You're a treasure, Talot."

"She'll be there in a minute, Talot. If you'll excuse us." Keirat's tone was firm.

"Of course, Master. Mistress." Talot nodded himself out the door.

Yes, it had indeed been a most satisfactory *Arraho*.

He smiled.

* * * * *

Keirat leaped from the bed, surprising Suliana. "Where are you going?"

He strode to the tray and examined the goblets. "Well, call me paranoid if you want, but I'm not taking any chances. Not with you."

Suliana grinned. "Okay."

He moved to a wall and touched one stone, and she gasped as a portion slid to one side revealing a console similar to Parnulet's. "Good grief." She stared, openmouthed, at the array.

Keirat, busy with buttons and switches, let the comment pass. "If I can remember how to work this thing…"

Suliana slipped from the bed and came to stand beside him, legs only a little shaky, which was pretty damn good, all things considered. She steadied herself by leaning against him.

"Is this a communications center? To the *Rahanarat*?"

"Yes." Keirat nodded. "Haven't used it in a long time, though." He clicked more buttons. "Ah. There we are."

The screen flickered and an image appeared. Sorl Dralet stared at them, his eyebrows rising at the sight of his daughter, stark naked, plastered over an equally naked Noul Keirat.

"Uhh…" Suliana shrank behind Keirat.

Keirat, however, was nonchalant. "Good morning, *Dad*."

Suliana stuffed her fist in her mouth to stifle her laughter. Where the hell did *that* come from?

"Master." Dralet's tone was anything but cordial. "How may we be of assistance?" His eyes flickered to Suliana's face. "Is my daughter well?"

She smiled back at the screen. "Thank you, Father. Yes, I'm very well. Very well indeed."

There was a mumbled comment from somewhere behind Dralet. He frowned. "Never mind."

Suliana wondered what pithy comment that old devil Parnulet had made, but she wasn't going to get the chance to find out, since her father seemed intent on business this morning.

"What do you need, Noul Keirat?"

"Your help. We suspect our wine may have been tampered with." He raised a hand as Dralet opened his mouth. "We did not drink any. We'd simply like it checked."

Dralet nodded. "Place a few drops on the slide screen, please."

Keirat hunted around, muttered to himself, and finally found the right place. He sprinkled a few drops from each goblet on the glass slide. "The right is from Suliana's. The left is from mine." He paused. "Uh…that's *my* right, of course."

Dralet rolled his eyes. "Yes."

Suliana grinned again, the smile that lingered around her mouth originating from somewhere deep inside. She pressed herself against the firm masculine back, and wickedly slid her hands around him.

He cleared his throat.

"I have the data." Dralet turned away from the screen and worked his equipment.

Suliana let her hands roam, and worked her mate's equipment.

Keirat squirmed. "Stop that." He hissed the words from the side of his mouth even as his cock leaped to life within her grasp.

"Just a moment, Master." Dralet snapped at the viewer without raising his head.

"Sorry." Keirat butted Suliana with his ass.

She giggled, burying her face against his spine and inhaling the scent of his skin. Daringly, she nipped at him, drawing blood, and then licking the pinprick closed.

"You *will* pay for that." He drawled the words quietly, head turned toward her, eyes alight.

She nodded politely. "I do hope so."

Keirat's expression heated. "Suli—"

"If you two have *quite* finished…" The acerbic tones of Dralet reverberated from the communications center. "I have some preliminary results."

"Ah." Keirat turned back to the screen and Suliana peeped around his shoulder. Involuntarily, her grasp on his cock tightened and he sucked in a quick breath.

Dralet, his sight thankfully limited to the small viewscreen, misunderstood. "It's not of major concern, Keirat. One sample has indeed been contaminated. But only with a simple tranquilizer, one quite common on Raheen. Our sensors picked it up immediately."

Suliana released Keirat. *Shit.* Somebody had tampered with their wine. "Whose goblet, father?"

"Keirat's. The tranquilizer was intended for him." Dralet's lips curled into an expression of distaste. "Appalling business. Quite out of character for a Raheeni. I'm disgusted. To think we have sunk so low."

"I agree. It will be taken care of." Keirat's tone was firm. "My thanks, *Rahanarat* Sorl Dralet."

Dralet bowed his head in acknowledgement of the respectful title. "You have not used this device much, Noul Keirat, Master of Raheen. Let us hope you will have more recourse to contact us in the future."

"I believe I will, Dralet. As long as your wisdom is available to guide me." Keirat's words reverberated in Suliana. She knew what he was implying, what he was asking.

Had they isolated the bacteria? Found a way to eliminate it?

Dralet knew too. "I trust this will be the case. As of this moment, of course, none of us knows the future. But we are always...optimistic."

The screen went dark as Dralet ended his transmission.

"They will do it, Keirat." Suliana turned him to face her. "I know they will do it."

He looked at her and then ran a gentle hand down her cheek. "My Suli."

She turned her face and dropped a kiss in his hand. "My Master. My Keirat." *My life.*

Chapter Eleven

Keirat's thoughts were somber and troubled as they prepared themselves for the *Kyreeha*.

It was unavoidable, a part of Raheen tradition, and they'd already violated a big one by sharing *Arraho* so soon after her recovery. He didn't want to push his luck by violating any more. The last thing either of them needed was a challenge to *his* authority, along with the one involving Suliana.

He slipped into his formal Master's robe, absently buttoning the row of clasps that adorned the front. He understood now why she had screamed out the *Kyreeha* in the Glade.

He understood her independence, her absolute belief that the man in her life would be the right one, worthy of her devotion, her body and her love—maybe even her life. It was something inside her that was unique, possibly a part of the "other", but whatever it was, he loved her for it.

Only a woman of great strength and personal integrity would have dared to issue such a challenge. Only a woman like his Suliana.

And she deserved a Master who could protect her, but damned if he knew how.

"You're worrying." She entered, radiant in her lavender robe. "Don't."

"How can I not?" He opened his arms and she went readily into his embrace. "We are about to enter the Glade of Arraho where you will formally declare *Kyreeha*. The people of Raheen will expect me to stand for you and defend you against all comers."

"Me and my big mouth." She groaned and hid her face against him.

"You and your strong principles." He smiled and dropped a kiss on her hair. "You were damned if you'd surrender to me. I had to prove myself worthy."

"Oh you have. In spades." Lips grazed his bare chest between the edges of the robe.

"Still, we're bound to obey Raheen laws." He sighed and eased their bodies apart, pushing her into a chair and throwing her a look that ensured she stayed there.

"Now. Whoever drugged the wine, and we'll assume for lack of any better suspects that it was Chanda, will think I am...not up to my usual strength." He paced the floor. "And we are guessing that Chanda is going to accept the *Kyreeha* for herself, returning it to you. Making *you* prove that you are a worthy Mistress."

Suliana nodded. "Nothing like a little female liberation."

"What?"

"Never mind. Sorry. Go on."

"Chanda, for whatever reason, seems hell-bent on destroying you, Suli. Make no mistake, this is a woman who will kill."

Suliana shivered. "I know. I've seen her do it."

"And Raheen being Raheen, killing is...part of our nature. Not something we do very often, but it happens." He tapped his fingers on the desk. "If she kills you during *Kyreeha*, she will be lauded as a stronger Mistress. A better Mistress. I will be tainted by my choice of you for my mate, and thus my standing will be threatened. It'll be hunting season on the Master until I too am disposed of."

"Leaving nobody in Chanda's way." Suliana nodded, grasping the situation comprehensively, as Keirat knew she would.

"What do we do?" He turned to her, unafraid to ask the question of another for probably one of the first times in his life. This was what sharing *Arraho* with his Mistress could do. Halve his burdens and double his pleasure.

She thought. "We plot. We plan. We play *her* game with *our* rules." She glanced at him. "I suppose having sex is out right now?"

A quick chuckle was surprised out of him. "*Suli.*"

"Sorry. I just have this itch this morning." She licked her lips and grinned at him.

"We'll scratch it. We'll have the rest of our lives to scratch it." Keirat wanted to believe that. He wanted a life with Suliana, and peace — of the Raheen sort — on his world. Simple requests. Surely between the two of them they could figure out a way to achieve them.

Suliana pursed her lips. "So we play her game. She's expecting you to be woozy." Her eyes pierced him, blazing in their intensity. "Woozy is what you'll have to pretend to be, my Master."

He frowned. "While she's killing *you*? I don't think so."

"You have very little faith in my abilities, Keirat."

"I have seen her in action, Suliana. She loves to feed. She is very strong. For her, it's not about the sex. It's about the power of the kill. Do not forget what happened to Mayara."

"I haven't." Suliana's face was set in hard lines. "I shall never forget Mayara's death. Nor the way Chanda ignored your command and sent her past the portal."

"Exactly. That is not going to happen today. Not to you." He clenched a fist. "Do you believe that I could watch her torture you and drain the life from you? Without lifting a finger to stop it?"

Suliana rose from the chair and walked to him, resting her open palms on either side of his face. "It will not happen to me, Keirat. I have my own strengths. My own skills. Just because I've been…elsewhere for a while doesn't mean I've been idle."

"Suli…" His heart thudded at the thought of the danger she would be facing.

"Trust me, Keirat. We shall attend the *Kyreeha*. I shall answer Chanda's challenge. And I shall *win*. You are going to have to watch your back. Because although the challenge to me is front and center, your life is obviously on the line here, too."

He nodded. "Agreed."

"I have an idea, a weapon that I need. And one I haven't seen used in the Glade. It…I remember writing a novel, a story about it." She frowned. "It's real, at least to me. All I have to do is find one." She glanced up at him. "Because I know how to use it."

He blinked. "What is it?"

"The blood flower."

Keirat stared at her. "*Great ray of light*. I thought that was a legend."

"It is. And it isn't. The legend fueled my story. The one I wrote when I was…in her." She shook her head. "It's confusing. She's me, and I am her. We are one. And right now, I need those memories, that story. And I need that blood flower."

"Perhaps Adella would know something about it?"

"Or my father." Suliana shrugged. "We'll ask."

Keirat nodded, but wondered silently if asking would be enough. If the legendary blood flower would be enough. If not, if something happened to Suli, he would kill Chanda without a blink. He didn't care if it violated his planet's laws, got him into more trouble than he could imagine, or even resulted in his own death.

He cared about none of that. He only cared about one thing right now.

Suliana.

* * * * *

Chanda, on the other hand, cared about nothing at all except her overwhelming desire to rule. Kael Melet might be a good fuck and a strong arm, but she had no illusions about who would be the real power in their relationship. It would be *her*.

She flexed her arms, swinging them wide in front of her mirror, admiring the play of light over the muscles and the way her breasts followed her moves. Yes, she was strong. Strong enough to rule over Raheen. To take them from the stupidly agrarian society they had become and into a dominant force to be reckoned with. A force that would venture out and invade other worlds, rather than simply defend itself.

She saw her body, lean and sensual, powerful in spite of its obviously feminine attributes. And she saw past it to the steel core of her, the part that demanded to be in control, in charge. The part that wanted to put its heel on the stupidly soft Raheeni and grind them to dust.

She was a warrior. Had her people forgotten the *true* meaning of the word? It was definitely time to remind them.

Sounds from her small suite distracted her. The servants were up and around, and Kael Melet had already left to prepare for the *Kyreeha*.

Chanda was ready. She was also bored. She needed something to pass the time.

She needed to fuck, and to feed. To energize her body and her strength. To drink deeply of someone, add their essence to her own. To suck the very life from them if need be.

She felt the hunger course through her veins like liquid fire. Grabbing her robe, she crossed the room, opening the door to the chamber beyond.

Two servants were tidying things, folding things, and making themselves useful. Chanda didn't appreciate their work. She did, however, appreciate their appearance.

She licked her lips as she stared past the simple tunics to the bodies beneath. Both males, they were young, hard and seemed strong. Just the way she liked her playthings.

Mmm. This was going to be fun.

"Good morning." A sensual purr of greeting startled the two men. They nodded respectfully.

Chanda lifted her hands to her head and then stretched them skyward. "Isn't it a lovely morning?" Her robe parted, slithering across her body to reveal her naked breasts.

"Yes…yes indeed." One young man swallowed as he tried not to look. The other just looked.

Chanda ran her hands down over her body, toying with her nipples and then barely brushing her hands over the dark pelt of her mound. "I'm bored and lonely." She pouted. "Will you play with me?"

"*W-w-with you?*" The longhaired man stuttered as his jaw dropped.

Chanda nodded. "With me." Her gaze drank in the other man, his hair shorter, but his body broader. "And *him.*"

Their expressions were almost identical, unsure and nervous. But their cocks stirred beneath the tunic. Oh yes. *That* part of their bodies was more than willing.

She strolled over to the first man, reaching to stroke his long hair. "What's your name?"

"Sakat, Madam." He sighed as she tugged a lock of hair.

He sighed even more when she reached to his groin and gripped his length. "You are built very nicely, Sakat. I like a hard cock." She stroked it, then released it as he moaned a little.

"And you?" Her question embraced the other servant.

"Reinet, Madam." He stared boldly back at her.

"Good, Reinet, good." Chanda ran her hand across his shoulders, then ripped his tunic from neck to hem. He did not move, but his cock swelled most satisfactorily.

Chanda smiled. "You'll do very well indeed." She walked to her desk and picked up her whip, turning to them. "Strip."

With alacrity, the two dropped their robes, shooting excited looks at her and each other.

She flicked her wrist and the whip cracked, making them both jump. "Do you like pain? Hmmm?" Another flick and a little red weal appeared on Reinet's chest. He choked and nodded, cock reddening.

Chanda smiled and slipped her robe off. The air felt good against her naked skin.

"And how about you?" She curled the length of the leather thong around Sakat's cock and tugged, bringing a cry bubbling from his throat.

"Yesss...oh yessssss..." He threw his head back and reached down to cradle himself.

"Oh, let *me*." Chanda bent and licked him, her tongue soothing the hurt and teasing his cock as he shifted his weight and thrust his hips toward her. "Mmm. Very tasty. Sweet."

She knelt on all fours and sucked Sakat deeply into her mouth, slurping her lips around him then pulling free. "You. Reinet. The paddle. Ever used one?"

He nodded. "Yes, Madam."

"Good. Use it now." She waggled her ass. "On me."

Obediently, Reinet picked up the paddle from her desk and hefted it in his hand, apparently feeling the weight of the hard leather flap as it moved in response to his wrist.

"Sometime this week?" Chanda returned to Sakat's cock, ass cheeks in the air.

There was a slap, and Chanda freed her lips. "Harder, man. You're not swatting flies. You're swatting *me*. I want to feel it. Make me *ache*, Reinet."

Sakat trembled and he seemed unsure of what to do, but she ignored him, simply sucking his sizeable cock back into her mouth and waiting.

Once again, the paddle hit her, but with a good amount of force this time. *Oh yes. Oh so good.* "Mmmm." She hummed around the cock in her mouth and sucked harder. Reinet repeated his stroke, again and again, smacking her and making her ass burn with the pain of his blows.

It was wonderful, firing up the hunger that possessed her and forcing her onto the cock she was sucking. "Lie down, Sakat." She grabbed his legs, ripping his thighs with her sharp nails and licking at the blood flowing over his skin.

She pulled him all the way down, straddled him, and shot a glance at Reinet. "Don't stop."

On all fours over Sakat now, she dangled her breasts over his face. "Bite me. Use your fangs. I want your desire." She teased his lips with her nipples. "Do it, Sakat. Pleasure me with pain."

Reinet kept up his flogging, slapping her forcefully, making her gasp with delight as the heat spread from her ass through her body. Her fangs emerged as her desire rose, and when Sakat daringly sucked a nipple into his mouth and pierced it with a fang, she cried out with joy.

This was the perfect playtime, two strong men at her beck and call, punishing her in all the ways she loved. Her arousal grew, hot wet juices flowing from her body to drench the man between her thighs.

Sakat moved, hands reaching for her, needy fingers fumbling around her pussy and finding her clit.

"Pinch it. *Hard.*" She muttered the words around her fangs, parting her thighs wide, welcoming the savage attack of the leather paddle even as she welcomed the sharp pain to her clit.

Both men were hot, their bodies radiating their excitement as they obeyed her, punished her and aroused her erotic nature.

She moaned, delighted with the assault of Sakat's fingers. She wrenched her nipple from his mouth, ripping the flesh and bleeding onto his lips. He licked her, frantically lapping at the wound, swallowing the hot blood and thrusting his hips upwards in an attempt to fuck her.

The blows to her ass stopped and teeth replaced them, ripping down over the softness of one cheek.

"*Aaaaargh.* Yessss…"

Chanda felt her skin split and open as more blood flowed, this time into Reinet's hungry mouth. He sucked and licked and bit again, each attack driving her higher, making her wetter and hotter. He pulled her cheeks roughly apart, thrusting a finger into her anus as he bit once more.

Great ray, these two were *magnificent*. Why hadn't she thought to try them before?

Sakat's hands slid to her breasts and he crushed them, squeezing them cruelly as she sobbed out a laugh of pleasure.

"I want to fuck you…" A hard cock thrust against her ass. "Please. Let me fuck you."

It was Reinet, behind her, dripping liquid from his fangs onto her skin and rubbing his cock around the juices that leaked profusely from her cunt.

"Me too." Sakat squeezed her breasts together and bit down, one fang catching each breast and sending a bolt of savage lust down Chanda's body to land straight on her clit.

She ached and throbbed and could've cried with the simple pleasure of it.

"Yes, *yes*…fuck me. Both of you. *Fuck* me…" She snarled the command, secure in the knowledge that it would be obeyed. She would not have to wait, suffer any prolonged delay, although sometimes that was even better.

Right now she wanted fucking. A good, thorough fucking.

Sakat's hands released her breasts and grabbed her hips, bending her at the right angle.

Reinet's hands joined his, spreading her ass cheeks wide, oh-so wide, pulling at her delicate ring of muscles as he dropped to his knees behind her.

With exquisite precision and no finesse whatsoever, the two cocks plunged in, huge and swollen and making Chanda feel like she was about to be ripped apart.

It was *wonderful.*

She howled with pleasure, filled to capacity with one cock thrusting into her cunt and another ravaging her ass.

In concert they moved, in and out, back and forth, Sakat pinching her nipples with sharp nails, and Reinet slapping her ass, sharp blows with his hand that simply added to her exquisitely erotic pain.

Hotter than fire, their bodies burned around her, breath coming in hisses past fangs that leaked desire.

"Feed on me, boys." Chanda threw her head back, bouncing fiercely from the power of their bodies, their thrusts.

Sakat opened his mouth and bit down on a breast, ripping it open to the hard nipple and sucking.

Reinet leaned into her and found her neck. He thrust his fangs deep as he thrust his cock deep—and Chanda screamed again at the enormous burst of pleasure growing within her cunt.

The fire in her blood erupted as she was fucked so thoroughly, devoured by such enthusiastic passion and surrounded by frenzied male heat. Sakat broke first, easing her breast from his mouth and licking at her, a glazed look stealing over his eyes.

His cock hammered into her, forced deep into her cunt by strong muscles and a stronger desire to explode.

Chanda watched him through eyes misted with a veil of blood. How sweet he was. How good a fuck he was. A groan behind her reminded her that the cock in her ass was swelling too.

Her fangs lengthened and her hunger began. The hunger that walked side by side with her orgasm, linked closer than close.

She was coming, as were her playmates. Sparks of electric current ran from her ass to her clit to her brain. Sakat cried out beneath her and pierced her cunt so sharply that she lifted up from the floor—pushing herself onto Reinet's cock at the same time.

It was all it took.

Each began the screaming descent into orgasm, Sakat writhing, fangs dripping and balls throbbing hard against her flesh. Reinet tore his mouth from her as his cock exploded in her ass, hot jets of come flooding her and overflowing down her thighs.

And Chanda took it all, her own spasms increasing in intensity, pulling at her, blinding her with her need to release the volcano within her.

She cried out as it began, great shudders streaking across her body, shattering her and blinding her with pleasure.

Her head dropped, her fangs found skin and she let go, tearing into Sakat with the viciousness born of an orgasm too mighty to be restrained.

She drank and ripped and drank again, greedy and unsated as he collapsed beneath her. Her cunt clenched hard around his softening cock, and she snarled out a curse, reaching for Reinet.

He tried to pull away but she was too quick, too strong for him.

Within seconds, his blood, his flesh was prolonging the orgasm, sending Chanda once again into the realms of this insane pleasure. She fed voraciously, fueling the fire with the essence of her playmates.

Her cunt contracted, thunderous waves of climactic delight that shook her to her core. It was incredible, wonderful, and what she'd wanted so badly this morning.

Finally, it eased, leaving her sated and refreshed and sitting amongst the bloody and unconscious bodies of Sakat and Reinet.

She blinked.

Oh dear. What a shame.

Chapter Twelve

Darkness was falling over the Glade of Arraho as Suliana and Keirat made their way through the arch and into the sheltered arena. Suliana looked around curiously — it was her first time seeing it through her own eyes, not in some dream vision.

Tall trees circled the grassy lawn, stone arches linking the ancient trunks and forming a rough circular clearing. The sky soared above, and later would fill with the light of Raheen's two moons. But for now, only a few early stars were twinkling and the haze of dusk obscured much of the view.

At the far end, on an altar sort of thing, the delicate Raheen *Kyreeha* Axe was shining. A token representation of the challenge to take place, it had been hurriedly removed from its repository beneath the surface of the planet, cleaned, and placed prominently on display.

And Suliana had to admit it was quite beautiful, the jewels glowing in the slim silver handle, and the twin blades sparkling at one end. Its history was lost to time, but its existence reinforced the traditions that had ruled Raheen as strongly as its Masters.

She drew in a breath and squared her shoulders as she walked beside Keirat to the two chairs placed beneath an arch. Elsewhere around the Glade were the toys of Raheen sexual pleasure. She glimpsed bars, chains, the distinct X-shaped trestle, and several low benches.

It was all familiar, yet new to her, and part of her mind was completely fascinated. The other part was whirring with plans, considering various ideas and scenarios.

They had the blood flower. It lay in the box carried reverently by Talot, and would be exposed at the appropriate moment.

Keirat had finally been persuaded to mimic the effects of a tranquilizer, although it had been a hard battle to win. Suliana had talked herself blue in the face trying to make him see the wisdom of such a course.

Fortunately, he'd agreed two minutes before she'd grabbed the nearest rock and smacked him upside the ear with it, seriously screwing with Raheen and all its male supremacy traditions.

Talot and Adella had helped. Keirat had agreed they were probably the only two who could be trusted, and Chanda's plotting wouldn't come as news to them, anyway. But the rest of the Raheeni gathered that night knew nothing of the undercurrents swirling around the Master and his Mistress. They were simply there to watch the excitement of a *Kyreeha*, and fuck themselves silly afterwards.

They had no idea what lay ahead. And for that matter, neither did Suliana. It was all guesswork, assumptions, masquerades and a healthy dose of prayer.

She took her seat next to Keirat, carefully arranging her robe. They were the only ones wearing clothes, a fact which made Suliana oddly self-conscious. As if by their concealment, they were setting themselves apart from the other Raheeni.

A stir across the Glade caught Suliana's eye, and she looked over to see Chanda elbowing her way to the front of the throng.

It was time.

She glanced at Keirat as he stood and raised his hand for silence.

"Raheeni, I am Noul Keirat, your Master. I declare my intention to take Suliana as my Mistress. She has chosen this path of her own free will."

He swayed a little and put a hand to his head, then shook it, and continued. "As is her right, Suliana has called *Kyreeha*. She has agreed to abide by the result."

Chanda stepped forward, followed by Kael Melet.

"*I* will answer her challenge, Master." Chanda stood tall, alone in the rising moonlight. Her body glowed, muscles gleaming, hair streaming over her shoulders. She was vibrant, strong, and quivering with barely suppressed energy. Her breasts rose and fell with her breaths, twin mounds topped by dusky nipples, glittering a little as if she'd dusted them with starlight.

"You have a champion to suggest?" Keirat looked past her. "Kael Melet?"

"You misunderstand, Master." Chanda's words were respectful, but her eyes were full of fire. "*I* will answer the challenge."

"You? *You* will meet the Mistress's champion?" Keirat poured astonishment into his voice.

"You're overacting." Suliana hissed the words from beside him under cover of a cough.

He ignored her, merely continuing to stare at Chanda.

Who smiled. "Oh no, Master. I wish to accept Suliana's challenge and face *her*. I wish to fight Suliana. Winner take all." She ignored the buzz of mutterings that rapidly spread through the crowd. "If she's brave enough."

Chanda's final words were spoken loudly enough to ring from tree to archway, and none could miss her meaning, her own challenge. *Did Suliana have enough guts to be Mistress?*

It was stunning, silencing the Raheeni as they held their breath. Nothing like this had occurred in recent memory, and Suliana let the moment linger before moving. She knew the value of a dramatic pause.

Then she rose. Standing tall next to Keirat, Suliana deliberately unfastened the robe and allowed it to fall to the floor around her feet. Naked, she stared at Chanda, anger flooding her at this *bitch* who dared to scheme and lie in order to get what she wanted.

Power. It was all about power.

And Suliana wasn't about to give any to a woman she knew was a vicious killer. "*I accept.*"

* * * * *

Keirat swallowed, fighting the urge to walk onto the grass, sink his fangs into Chanda and rip her throat out. His fury knew no bounds.

Neither did his pride in his mate as she stood naked beside him, proudly facing a dangerous foe and meeting the threat head-on. Her eyes glittered with that strange assortment of colors as she faced him.

"Master, with your permission…"

He nodded, feeling helpless, frustrated, and for the first time in his life, afraid he was going to lose the thing he loved most.

Keirat had met challenges throughout his existence—he'd fought his way to the role of Master, and done his best to honor the title. He'd been weak, furious, injured and happy on occasion.

He'd never experienced fear before. Not like this.

Never had he felt chills running up his spine, or a light sweat beneath his arms at the mere thought of a battle. There was no heated adrenaline rush, no extension of the fangs in readiness for the conflict.

This wasn't his conflict, and yet—it was. Suliana was his mate. His heart, if not his very soul. Trusting that she would triumph was taxing his abilities to their limits and beyond. But he knew that he must allow this…this…abomination to take place, or ruin what chances they had of restoring Raheen to rights.

The plans were underway to decontaminate the water, to remove the alien bacteria that had slowly poisoned the wells.

Now it was time to remove a woman who had done as much to poison Raheen in her way as any alien plague.

Chanda had followers. Young people who had been seduced by her sexuality, her violence, her strength. Should Suliana fail, there was no doubt in Keirat's mind that Chanda would overthrow them all.

Chaos would result, without question. Even with the plague gone, and that was still only a possibility, Chanda's brand of rule would surely send Raheen down the road to ruin.

Suliana moved from his side and crossed to face Chanda. "I accept. I will meet you in combat." Her voice was calm and level, her bearing erect. "And I shall give no quarter."

There was an outbreak of murmurs at her words. *No quarter* meant just that. A fight to the death. This would not be the fucking and feeding of the *Arraho*. This would transcend sex and take the two women back into Raheen's distant past, when fighting and combat included fangs. And certain death.

"My weapon, *Tapa-hir*." Suliana turned and beckoned Talot, who respectfully walked to her side and presented the box.

Chanda's eyes followed his hands as he raised the lid. "What the…" She frowned. "That is no weapon." A sneer passed across her face. "I should have known one such as you would pretend to fight. Trickery. Mere trickery."

She turned away as Suliana lifted the blood flower from its silken nest. "Are you *quite* sure?"

She shook out the lashes and squared her shoulders.

Keirat held his breath, knowing from her stance she was preparing herself.

Suliana raised her arm, the braided leather handle held firmly in her grasp. Dozens of leather lashes cascaded from the tip, each one ending at a slightly different length in one black leather flower.

And each lash peppered with sharp fangs—like thorns, small, and woven into the leather.

They bit into Chanda as Suliana's arm moved like lightning, her wrist flicking the thongs across her opponent's back. Tiny droplets of blood appeared, running over her skin, blending, mixing into a stream across the firm body.

Chanda screamed and turned, reaching out for her whip and unfurling it as it was passed to her.

Suliana bared her teeth and let her fangs show as she circled Chanda. "*Kyreeha, you motherfucking bitch.*"

The battle had begun.

* * * * *

With the first whistling lash of the blood flower, Suliana felt a cold fury of emotion settle over her brain. A desire to punish, to *eliminate*, this crawling worm from the surface and the consciousness of Raheen.

Chanda was quick, though, her whip flying free and catching Suliana on the thigh, ripping the flesh and making her bleed in her turn. There was no pain, just anger. No rush of desire, just a solid need to…to *kill*. To protect that which was hers. And Noul Keirat was *hers*.

The onlookers drew back, forming a circle, a theater-in-the-round of blood, silently watching the two women size each other up.

Suliana had Chanda's measure. She had to keep her off-kilter, if possible. Do the unexpected, respond with the unexpected, and generally confuse her. She could not afford to show weakness, pain or any reaction to Chanda's blows.

Or her words.

"Filthy whore. You *dare* to think *you* can be Mistress of Raheen?" Chanda spat the words and followed them with a flurry of lashes, most of them landing somewhere on Suliana.

"You think you're good enough to mate with the Master?" More lashes followed, in the same pattern, right, then left. Chanda had a predictability to her moves that Suliana was learning very quickly.

She took the blows, ignoring the small wounds and the blood that dappled her naked body. And she ignored the venom spewing from Chanda's lips.

Her own fangs lengthened as she gathered her strength, waiting — waiting — until the second of the maneuvers was recoiling.

Now. The blood flower flew through the air between them, catching Chanda on the neck and shoulder and pulling away pieces of flesh as Suliana tore it free.

Chanda's mouth opened on a yell, and her fangs dripped, healing liquids that were inadequate to the task. It was a damaging blow and Chanda knew it, since she retreated a little, out of range of those vicious thongs.

"Scared yet, *bitch*?" Suliana flicked her arm, letting the flowers spray in an oddly beautiful arc through the air. "Worried you might fall before a *weak whore*?" She moved closer, forcing Chanda backward. "Frightened you might *lose*? Die right here in front of all those you've fooled into believing you're some kind of sex-queen?"

Chanda's eyes narrowed. "I am who I am. A Raheeni. A strong Raheeni. We fuck and we feed. It is our way." She lifted her arm, signaling yet another attack. "I wouldn't expect a weakling like you to understand."

The lash whistled, and Suliana again ignored the blows, although one across her breast made her wince as her nipple split and bled freely.

The ground was getting slippery beneath Suliana's feet. And part of her knew she couldn't keep accepting such blows without suffering some sort of consequence. She pushed down her pain, spared a moment's thought for Keirat, and drew strength from his image as it flickered across her brain.

"I *am* the Mistress of Raheen, Chanda." She caught the woman a solid hit across the abdomen, ripping her from hip to navel. "I *am* the mate of the Master." Another blow, another line of blood. "The Master you attempted to *poison*."

Chapter Thirteen

Keirat's senses went on high alert at Suliana's revelation, since a low cry of horror and disbelief spread through the assembled Raheeni.

"Watch yourself, Keirat." Suliana yelled the words as she defended herself from a violent attack, Chanda unleashing everything she had into the fight.

Keirat moved swiftly to one side, and only just in time, since a sharp dagger had whistled perilously close to his chest. He looked for, and found, Kael Melet.

The man was staring, his mouth open, his eyes wide, unable to comprehend that his supposedly drugged target had moved so quickly.

His momentary immobility was his undoing, since to attack the Master in an underhanded and devious way was not acceptable by *any* Raheen standards. Challenge was one thing, assassination another. Hands grabbed Melet and held him, although he fought to free himself.

Keirat was torn. He needed to take care of his end of things, but could not ignore the fight still going on in the center of the Glade.

Fortunately his people responded, angrily at first and then in typical Raheen fashion. They tore into Kael Melet, his blood feeding them, stirring them into a frenzied level of arousal and lust. Within moments, fangs appeared, bloodied in the body of Melet, and then sinking deep into a partner, while many couples surrendered *Arraho*.

The moons were high, the passions running even higher, and the excitement of the challenge had aroused the most basic sexual natures of the Raheeni crowd. They fucked, fed, and fucked again, oblivious to the challenge between Suliana and Chanda.

Melet's betrayal and death had unstoppered the bottle of violent passion that formed the core of the Raheen vampire race. Blood, sex and passion walked together, combining into a unique species that survived by courting death in the throes of desire.

And still the women fought.

Keirat hesitated. Should he stop it? Should he step in and end the combat now? The threat to him was past. The threat to Suliana still stood in the Glade, whip in bloody hand, and fangs sharply bared.

His people might be lost in their own lusts, but they would not miss the eventual outcome of the *Kyreeha*. He was caught, caught by Raheen traditions, caught by his love for his mate, and pulled savagely between the two. It was a torture of unbelievable agony, and Keirat choked down a cry of warning as Chanda once again lunged at Suliana.

Both women were bleeding freely, and he ached to run to his mate. He wanted to heal her, lick her wounds, taste her blood and fuck her blind, just to reassure himself she was still alive. Still his.

A sharp crack from Chanda's whip stopped his heart, and a long weal appeared down one of Suliana's cheeks. It was the last straw.

She unleashed a torrent of sharp attacks, peppering Chanda's body with viciously rapid lashes. Her hand moved so quickly it was a blur, and even some of the Raheen paused in their fucking to watch, mouths dropping at Suliana's skill.

Keirat forced himself to stand still, to ignore the remains of Melet, a bloody heap on one side of the Glade. He forced himself to ignore the wounds to his mate. He forced himself to be what he was. The *Master* of Raheen.

And to let Suliana prove she was, indeed, its Mistress.

* * * * *

Lost in the battle, Suliana spared barely a thought for anyone or anything else. She'd seen Keirat dodge the knife, knew he was safe, and that was all that mattered.

Now it was between her and Chanda.

And her and herself. The two parts of her nature warred within her brain even as her body attacked, defended and attacked once more. Her skill was pure Raheen, her aim deadly. The fact that none of the blows had been fatal was a product of the other part of her, the more compassionate part, the part that she'd retained when she "came home".

Trying to reconcile her conflicting emotions was taking its toll every bit as much as the lashes from Chanda's whip, and it was damned clear that Chanda was good with her weapons. She meant to kill Suliana, no doubt about it.

With her face on fire, blood sliding across her naked body and her lungs heaving, Suliana began to force Chanda backward. There was no letup in her slashing lunges. The thorns of the blood flower dripped with glittering maroon droplets, clear proof that she was striking home, weakening Chanda with each blow.

No more vicious weapon had ever been invented on Raheen. It had fallen out of favor for use in the Glade, since it left the recipient in no shape for an enthusiastic fucking afterwards. But Suliana's father had kept one, and right at this moment she was extremely glad he had, since she knew that without it, she would have succumbed to Chanda's extraordinary strength and determination.

"She could beat me. She's strong enough to win."

I know.

Suliana's mind spoke to itself, an inner dialogue punctuated by slashing swipes of her forearm. Her shoulders were beginning to do some serious aching.

"I must triumph. For Raheen."

Yes. You must.

For the first time, Chanda stumbled, catching herself up on the stone altar that dominated one end of the Glade. She hissed through her fangs and renewed her attack. Truly this woman was indomitable. Her strength was almost unheard of, even for Raheen.

"Do you think she's…?"

Could be. How could we tell?

There was nothing in Chanda's outward appearance to suggest she was anything alien, anything other than Raheeni. And she certainly bled like one.

In a surprise move, Chanda dashed forward, tossing her whip away, dodging beneath the lashes of the blood flower and throwing herself onto Suliana.

Two fangs ripped into her skin, tearing strips of flesh from neck to breast and Suliana felt the urge to wrench free of this ghastly mouth. *"I must get her off me."*

But if she feeds from you she will become immune. The plague will have one less victim.

"Can we afford a healthy woman – of her nature?"

I cannot answer that. But you know what our blood can do. This time, it is you who must choose.

However, the choice was taken out of Suliana's hands.

Chanda tore herself away and spat, a bloody spume of Suliana's flesh and liquids spewing from her lips and spattering on the soft turf. "I will not foul my mouth or my body with one such as you." There was truly no end to her hatred.

"You weaken, Chanda. Let us stop this. Now." Suliana offered her hand as Chanda swayed and fell to her knees.

"Maybe you are right." Chanda's voice was low and she reached to her head as if in pain. "Maybe it *is* time to end it."

Swiftly she pulled something from her hair—a sharp and deadly blade no longer than her finger. Mustering her strength she flung it at Suliana. *Straight* at Suliana.

A horrified silence had fallen over the Glade, and for Suliana time slowed to a surreal blur. The soft purple light of Raheen's twin moons turned the shining knife into a twinkling flash of beautiful danger as it winged its way to Suliana's head.

Move. Move now.

She obeyed her inner voice and swayed, a small shift, but enough. The blade whistled past, severing a few hairs and dusting her cheek with a breath of air. It fell harmlessly to the ground behind her.

Chanda cried out in anger and toppled to the ground. "No. No *way* can you win. You may *not* survive me. I am the *strongest*. I shall *kill* you."

"*I cannot let her live.*"

I know. You must do what is right for Raheen. We will do what is necessary.

Suliana's hand found the cool handle of the *Kyreeha* axe, and her fingers closed around it. Without conscious volition, she swung it from its resting place and up, up…over her head, securing it with both hands as she stared at Chanda.

"You accepted the *Kyreeha*."

"Wait…I…"

"You lost. To me."

"*Never*." Chanda refused to surrender even when looking death in the eyes.

"You betrayed the Master, attempted to assassinate him, and violate the Challenge with a hidden weapon." Suliana tensed her muscles and firmed her grip on the axe. "You fucking *cheated*, you bitch."

"And I'll do it again if I have to." Defiantly, Chanda ignored the blood flowing from the myriad of wounds on her body, pooling around her in ever-increasing stains which darkened the turf.

"No, you won't. Not *ever* again." Suliana raised her eyes to the Master for one small moment, drawing courage from his dear face, so full of concern and horror at the battle.

"This is for Mayara. For the Master. For *Raheen*. I claim *Kyreeha*." Suliana swung the heavy blade down, feeling the weight of the sharp edges part the air as it fell. Her aim was accurate — and deadly.

As she let the blade fall, Chanda's breasts heaved as she sucked in air. She pushed herself upwards in one final desperate attempt to fight back. It was the wrong thing to do. She met the oncoming blow and doubled its force.

With one crushing hit, Suliana cleaved Chanda's breastbone, shattering her ribs and splitting her nearly in two. The combined forces of both women crushed bones, sliced flesh and organs, and laid Chanda open from neck to navel.

It was the death blow.

"I had to do it. There was no other choice."

For a moment, Suliana heard nothing but the silence of the Glade. And felt a huge and overwhelming sorrow at the realization she had taken a life.

Then her mind responded and the sorrow eased.

I know. And I understand. I am you and you are me. We are one. We have chosen.

* * * * *

Keirat caught her as she fell.

His arms enfolded a bloodied and wounded Suliana, pulling her close even as his tongue swept her wounds. His pride in her had increased beyond belief, and his respect for her soared to incredible heights.

Only he knew the terrible price her act would cost her. Only he had fed from her and knew the depths of her compassion, her love…her all-consuming desire to protect him and Raheen. And even he could not guess at the level of spiritual pain she would experience at such a savage slaying.

The knowledge made him even gentler as he healed the whip slashes, laying her down beside him, ignoring the rest of the Glade in his efforts to soothe her. Soft murmurs came and went, the Raheeni cleaning up the mess the Challenge had left behind, and restoring everything to rights.

To Keirat's surprise, a couple of women knelt beside Suliana and tentatively lowered their heads, adding their own tongues to the healing efforts.

He nodded, giving his approval.

"Mistress." The word was respectful, almost devout, and as one woman left, another would take her place. It was homage, a way of acknowledgement, of confirming Suliana's position as Mistress.

And it was almost unreal—something that had not occurred for as long as Keirat could remember. The hairs on his skin lifted even as he healed Suliana, sharing that loving task with other Raheeni.

This demonstration of...affection, of respect...well, it was unexpected and surprising, not to mention extremely unusual for his race. But then again, this was Suliana. She was about the most unusual woman of his race he could have imagined.

And she healed rapidly. With the attentions of so many, the savage wounds were sealed, her blood cleansed from her skin and her body restored to health. Finally, her eyes opened, seeking his and glowing with a smile as she found him.

"*Keirat.*"

Only one word, but it was enough. He wanted to howl his joy to the skies, but choked back the sound. It would not do for the Master to show such weakness. He settled for holding her closely, and brushing his hand down the side of her face. "Suliana. You are well?"

She nodded. "Good. Real good." Her eyes with their oddly brilliant colors glowing fire at him, smiled. "Hungry though."

He grinned back. "And what are you hungry for?"

The lavenders and blues mingled around the dark pupils as they dilated. He knew what her answer would be even as she opened her mouth.

"You."

"Good answer." Noul Keirat, Master of Raheen and possessor of a rather awesome erection, even by *his* standards, sighed in satisfaction. "*Very* good answer."

Chapter Fourteen

Suliana's thoughts whirled and her heart was confused as she watched Keirat take control of the Raheen in the Glade.

He passed the word along to clear away the "debris", and what was left of Chanda disappeared as if by magic. Nobody wanted to feed on her, in fact they touched her with expressions of distaste.

Could she be the alien who had poisoned them? Suliana thought it likely. But then Keirat returned and she forgot everything but him.

"Well, my Mistress. Our people are expecting us to share *Arraho*. What do you say?"

She thought for a moment, letting Keirat sweat it out. "Okay." No sense in keeping him waiting *too* long.

He reached for her but she stayed him with her hand.

"*But…*"

He groaned even as he dropped his robe to the ground. "But *what*?"

"But in all honesty, I don't think I'm up to the whole punishment thing." She looked at him. "I'll probably disappoint the entire frickin' planet, but I swear if anyone so much as sneezes on me, I'll cry."

His eyes narrowed. "Are you sure you're all right?"

"Yes." She snuggled into him, loving the way his arms automatically cradled her. "I'm more than all right. But I know my limitations." She nipped his arm, sipped a little of his delicious blood, and then licked at the pinprick. "Your blood strengthened me, Keirat. I could never have withstood her without it. But it took everything I had...everything *we* had...to win."

"And it took more than blood and strength, didn't it?" He played with her fingers. "It took a decision. A choice. You chose to kill, even though you didn't want to."

"You understand." Suliana was surprised.

"Yes. I understand. When we shared *Arraho*, Suli, I sensed something in you that was unique. A compassion, a warmth, a need to help others. It...it...*astounded* me. It warmed me in strange places." He frowned at their intertwined hands. "I can't describe it or comprehend it, but it feels...*right*."

"Damn straight." She giggled. "Um...I guess I'm going to be Mistress, then, huh?"

Keirat tilted his head to one side and looked at her, sending heat through her blood and making her fangs ache. "There was never any doubt."

Great ray, how I adore this man.

"Then, Master, I think I'd better speak those words I never really thought I'd mean." She slid her body against his, uncaring of the other Raheen who might be watching. "I surrender."

Keirat reached around her, grabbing her ass and pulling their flesh together in all the right places. "I accept."

He kissed her, careful not to scratch her with his fangs, although within seconds she wanted him to. He was gentle, sensual and subtle, arousing her with touches, little nips, licks and caresses.

There was a murmur from the crowd, and Suliana laughed, glancing around to see others imitating Keirat. Apparently it was quite a success to judge from the surprised and pleased sounds.

"Perhaps we'll save the toys for special occasions." Keirat slid his fangs around her nipple, rubbing it with their hard edges and making her shiver.

"Oh, I don't know about that. I love the toys. I love the lash, especially when you wield it. I love the spankings, the cuffs and the blindfolds. I love everything you've ever done to me, Keirat. Everything you ever will do to me. In fact…" She grabbed his head and tipped it up so that she could look into his eyes. "In fact…I love you." She smiled. "Pretty dreadful, isn't it?"

"Yes. It's quite awful. We'll probably never live it down." Keirat smiled back. "But you know something?"

She shook her head, letting her fingers sift through the softness of his hair. "No, what?"

"This love? It's been missing. It's what Raheen needed. What I needed. To be a good Master, to make the right choices, the right decisions. We're a savage people living on a harsh planet. We're facing difficult times. Knowing now what it is to love somebody more than oneself…well, perhaps things will change." He licked one breast slowly, a long swipe of his tongue, and smiled against the soft swell. "Perhaps now we'll be able to move forward into the future with our passions, our desires, our savagery and something to temper them all into a greater strength."

"Love?"

"Mmm hmm."

"Aww. You old softie." She slithered her legs around his. "Don't let it get out, okay? I don't want my Master facing his own challenges every other Tuesday."

His cock rubbed her thigh. "Me neither. I plan on being very busy every other Tuesday." His teeth ran down her belly, leaving the faintest of lines behind them which he promptly licked dry. "Very busy indeed."

"Oh yeah?" Her fingernails scrabbled against his shoulders.

"Yeah."

"Doing what?" She parted her thighs, offering herself to him.

"This."

His mouth reached her pussy and he opened it wide, letting his tongue and his fangs part her soft folds as he lapped at the juices. A light nip, barely a sting, and Suliana sobbed out her delight as Keirat suckled from her clit. He teased her, toyed with her and made her weep healing tears from her fangs, salty tears from her eyes and hot tears of desire from her cunt.

He took his time, leading her higher, encouraging her, feeding from her now and again, always healing, always heating her with his tongue. He plunged it deep into her darkness, seeking more of her taste, pushing his face against her, fangs hard and thrust deep into her soft pussy.

"Keirat, oh *Keirat*..." She grabbed for him, tugging him away from her legs and up over her breasts. "I want you."

"You have me. All of me."

It was the right choice.

* * * * *

Keirat ached.

He wanted to bury his fangs deep in any part of Suliana he could reach and drink her dry. He wanted to thrust his cock deep into her body and his essence into her soul. But he held back, an unusual feat in and of itself, but a feat made easier by his concern for her. His *love* for her.

She'd fought with enormous skill and strength, but it had depleted her energies. Tonight, their *Arraho* would be slow and leisurely, and he didn't give a fuck who thought what about it.

What the hell good was being Master if you couldn't make your own rules now and again?

Besides, he found he was rather enjoying the chance to explore this woman, to make her writhe in pleasure from just the touch of his hands or his lips rather than the sting of the lash. He suckled her nipples, learned them with his tongue, then gently nipped and fed from them, letting her sighs and gasps of delight guide him.

And she sighed. And gasped. And when he touched her with his cock, just letting the swollen head graze her clit, she cried out. Damned if he didn't feel a yell coming on himself.

He swallowed it down. There was a time for yelling, and it wasn't quite yet.

Her pussy seared him, hot liquids telling him how aroused she was, how much she needed him. Her hands ran all over him, nails digging into his muscles, arousing him in his turn.

When Suliana found his buttocks and cupped them, he feared he would explode with the feel of her hot palms. In arousing her, he had aroused himself, and both were nearing fever pitch.

They had forgotten the challenge, the Glade, the Raheeni, the plague, and every single thing that might have distracted them. For this moment, there was only the two of them. Master and Mistress. Man and woman.

He settled himself between her thighs, letting her softness cradle his cock. They fit so well, merged so perfectly, and he was helpless to stop himself from seeking out her cunt. He *needed*. He needed so very badly.

And so he took what he needed. And with the taking, he gave in return.

Slowly, slower than he'd ever gone in his entire life, Keirat entered Suliana, his cock creeping into the slick silk of her cunt. She burned him, marked him forever, and he found himself staring into her eyes as he filled her.

Luminous colors flickered, lit by the fire of desire inside her that matched the flame in him. She was his, body and soul, and he claimed her, coming to rest with his body tight to hers, their hips touching, his cock nestling against her womb.

"*Ahhh, Suli.*" He breathed the words, scarcely realizing he spoke. His fangs were ready, needy, but still he held back, treasuring this unique moment in time.

"Keirat. I love you. I love being fucked by you. You are undoubtedly the best fuck in the galaxy. But if you don't fucking *move* within the next ten seconds, I swear I'll kill again." Suliana's eyes laughed at him, challenging him, as her hips pushed up against his.

He took the rather unsubtle hint and moved, slow strokes at first, then faster as Suliana's breath shortened and her neck arched. Their bodies met, sharp slaps of flesh against flesh, groin against clit, cock against womb.

"*Keirat*..." She hissed the words past fangs that shone with a light of their own.

"*Yesss*..." He felt it too, a shiver, a tremble, a bolt of excitement that began to sweep through him. It was time.

The second her cunt started to shudder around his cock, he found her flesh and sank his fangs deep. She lifted her head and found him, the sharp pain brought on by the penetration of her fangs sending him over the edge.

They locked to each other, a mass of orgasmic delight, the fluids flowing copiously between them. He tasted her, sweet and warm, and filled her with his come. Hot jets erupted as his balls emptied themselves into her, only to fill and empty again as he fed.

Her cries were muffled by his flesh, but he could feel her clamping down on him, ferociously squeezing his cock, her cunt boiling around him in ripple after ripple of sexual release. His blood flowed into her, fueling her climax, sending her once more into the abyss of pleasure.

It was endless wonder, explosive passion, and a totally incredible fuck. It stunned Keirat with its simplicity, and awed him with its joy.

Finally, when they withdrew their fangs, softly healed each other with loving tongues, Keirat looked at her once more, drowning in the softness of her gaze.

His cock softened within her, swimming now in the lake of their juices.

Suliana's gaze met his. And as she smiled at him, he *knew*.

They had created life.

Several months later…

Keirat strode through the caverns, a smile on his face although his mind was far from settled.

The news was good, overall. Thanks to the work of the *Rahanarat*, Raheen's water was once again pure. They'd even had a few rainstorms to lessen the drought, although it had been too little, too late, for this season's harvest.

Those privy to the information about the plague had concluded that Chanda had caused it. They didn't know how, and no longer cared. The threat had passed, the water was secure and more rain was anticipated, along with a solid winter snowfall in the mountains. The snowmelt would certainly raise the water levels next spring, if not right now.

However, with diligent management there would be enough, even for the new mouths that had appeared, to bring joy into the lives of Raheeni families. There had been more births this year than last, and that too was good.

The Raheeni were also entranced by the introduction of books that *everyone* could read. Just for fun. No longer were they weighty tomes suitable only for the education of would-be *Rahanarat*. Suliana had seen to that.

In a society where traditions and histories were passed down by word of mouth from generation to generation, the notion of actually *writing* anything other than an instructional manual was revolutionary, to say the least.

Suliana had eagerly written a few stories herself and encouraged other women to begin writing about…*stuff. Female stuff.* He'd tried to read it, but confessed himself rather at a loss with the heavy doses of romance he'd found. *Soppy stuff.*

He snorted. Give him a good battle any day. Perhaps he just ought to sit down and bloody well write one of his own. Something the average male Raheeni could get his fangs into. He shrugged as he turned toward his quarters.

For now, there were enough books...no—*novels*...to keep the women happy. The men would get their turn.

He hurried into his quarters, spurred on by a weak cry from within.

Oh great ray of light. *It was time.*

And indeed it was. Suliana lay on their bed, legs spread wide, whimpering now and again, as her swollen belly fluttered and convulsed. She turned her head as he came through the door to her side.

"You motherfucking sonovabitch. If I ever let you near me again with that goddamned cock of yours, I swear I'll throw myself on the nearest sword. Right after I've castrated *you*..." She grimaced and reached for his hand, squeezing it hard enough to stop his circulation.

He glanced worriedly at Adella, only to receive a calm smile. "All is proceeding normally, Master."

"Huh." Suliana grunted. "Easy for *her* to say." Her face contorted. "*Sheeeeiiiittt*..."

With the oath, her belly moved, and Adella urged her on, words of encouragement falling naturally into the gaps between Suliana's curses.

Shortly thereafter, a miracle occurred. At least it seemed like a miracle to Keirat.

He watched, speechless, as another life entered the room, pushed free of his mate's body on a gush of blood. Truly an appropriate entrance for a Raheen child. *His* child.

His heart stopped as the small squirming creature was wrapped and passed to him. He held it awkwardly at first, just looking at it.

"You have a beautiful daughter, Master Keirat." Adella smiled. "Congratulations."

"A daughter?" He stared at the mop of black hair that spiked on top of the small head.

"We have a daughter." Suliana's voice was ecstatic.

Keirat found his lips curving into a grin. "She's beautiful." He bent low to the bed, bringing his precious armful near his Mistress. "Look at her, Suli."

The little mouth pursed, then opened in a lusty cry. Tiny fangs peeped from her pink gums. She was a perfect Raheen child, in every way.

Suliana reached for her, holding her to her breast and offering her swollen nipple to the hungry mouth. Fortunately, the need to feed restricted itself to a simple suckling in the young of Raheen. There would be no desire to feed on anything other than milk or food for quite a few years.

Keirat watched, spellbound, as his daughter nursed at her mother's breast. It was truly a miracle of galactic proportions, and his heart swelled with pride and delight.

"You're smiling." Suliana's voice was light as she turned her head to him. "You're wearing what I would call a shit-eating grin, in fact."

"Am I?"

"Yeah. Very un-Master-like."

"Don't care." He reached out and brushed the soft downy cheek. "What shall we name her?"

The baby continued to suckle, but at the sound of his voice, she opened her eyes.

Both Suliana and Keirat gasped aloud.

The baby's eyes were quite blue, flecked with purple and lavender highlights. Truly her mother's daughter.

Suliana smiled. "Her name is Juli." She settled more comfortably against the pillows and Keirat's arm. "It's a kick-ass name, and I think it suits this young lady. She's gonna be a kick-ass broad…"

Keirat could only nod. Suliana was right.

This child was unique. He had no idea what she would grow up to be, or what effect she would have on Raheen and its people. She might be Mistress herself one day. Or a *Rahanarat*. But right at this moment, *kick-ass* sounded pretty good to him.

A slow smile crossed his face. "I'm...I'm..."

"Speechless?" Suliana chuckled.

"Yes."

Keirat realized he was. He had no words to express the emotions flooding him. He stared at his daughter as she stared soberly back.

And he realized that for once in his life, he didn't need words.

He had all he needed. He had love.

Epilogue

The news of the birth spread through the caverns with the speed of light, bringing smiles of shared joy to all who heard it. These days, any time a child was born was a good time. The birth of a child to the Master and his Mistress was cause for a major celebration.

And in traditional Raheen fashion, Talot had celebrated it between the thighs of his current woman. They'd shared a pretty fantastic *Tapaha* together, leaving Talot eagerly looking forward to the spring when they could take their affair to the next level and share *Arraho* on the surface of Raheen. The long hours of darkness and the reduced activity level always diminished the urge to feed, and although fangs appeared now and again, it was accepted that sex stayed just beneath the level of *Arraho* while the Raheeni remained beneath the surface of the planet.

Besides, it wouldn't be much fun to have to give birth just when one wanted to play, fuck, feed and generally let loose. Not to mention work the fields and harvests.

No, it worked better this way, mused Talot as he made his way to the quiet outer cavern he'd made his home.

He was tired. Bringing any woman pleasure for several hours was exhausting, and Shella had been pretty demanding. Of course, he'd met her demands, and made a few of his own.

Yes, she really had a very fine set of lips on her.

He grinned as he closed the door behind him, and threw his robe to the floor, tumbling into a lax heap of muscles on his bed. It had been a damned good night.

He yawned, stretched and closed his eyes.

A very good night...

He slept.

Some time later, the outlines of his body blurred and a light emanated from his limbs. Vaporous clouds swirled around Talot, sweeping from him in an incandescent stream. The particles solidified.

A being stood beside the bed looking down at the sleeping Raheeni from which it had just emerged.

I have failed.

It shook its head and unfurled soft wings, heaving a sigh of pleasure at the sensation. It was good to be free of the Raheeni form and stretch again.

Or have I? Could I have watched an entire species die? Again? Was it not bad enough to hear my own people's screams as their ships exploded? To know that in spite of their technology, their incredible intelligence, they were helpless?

It looked across the room at the small mirror and caught sight of its reflection.

Oh yes. I am myself once more.

Tall and lithe, he stood staring at his own image. Golden hair reflected the soft purple light in a strange way, and he smiled as his wings shifted delicately. He looked at himself as he really was—an invader. The last of his race. Oddly, the fact that he had tried to exterminate the Raheen people had not left a mark on his outward appearance. *I am out of place here on Raheen. It is time to leave.*

He knew they would survive. They were violent, savage, and had much to learn. But their new Mistress had brought new knowledge with her when her soul returned. And now there was a child who would advance the process. He would miss them both. She was a good woman, and of late he had become glad that his supply of contaminant was gone.

Too much death. Too much pain and anger. *I want to live again.*

Perhaps his futile attempt at revenge had left a mark after all. His blind anger at the Raheen, at the wanton destruction of his species' last hope for survival, had faded. He was overwhelmed for a moment with sadness. If only there had been some form of communication. If only…

He sighed as he realized he was thankful his plot had failed. Hatred like that could not be maintained, not when living as one of them, experiencing their lives, their hopes, their world. His species did not hate. They also did not love, not like the Raheen did. Not with every ounce of their being, every thought in their brains and every passion in their hearts.

Grief had mutated into anger. But the anger was gone. In its place was an emptiness that no amount of Raheen blood would fill.

Yes, it was time for him to leave. There were no others of his kind, no homeworld for him to return to. His soft green planet had been obliterated when their sun began the long journey to its death. It was the reason his people had taken to their ships in the first place.

I hunger.

He parted his lips and watched as fangs emerged. A corresponding stirring in his loins drew his attention and he smiled as his cock lengthened. He had "borrowed" the Raheeni male. He had *become* Talot, shared his thoughts, his desires, his fears, his pain and his pleasure.

And they had become part of him. A part that would travel with him wherever the winds of the galaxy blew him. His first stop would be a crypt deep below, where lights marked the trails of the Raheeni Mistresses' souls.

He knew how to use their transport device.

He would find a new home.

And once there I will feed.

Enjoy this excerpt from
The Sun God's Woman
© Copyright Sahara Kelly 2002

Prologue

The lights in the conference room dimmed and the polite babble of conversation diminished to an expectant hush. The dulcet tones of the moderator swirled around the guests.

"Ladies and gentlemen, it is my pleasure to present our keynote speaker this evening. From Pendrake Industries, here to tell us about his exciting new discoveries, may I ask you to join me in welcoming Dr. Kyle Pendrake."

An enthusiastic round of applause greeted this comment, and in the back row of the room Annie Lynden caught her breath.

He was gorgeous.

He was one hot babe-magnet whose pictures hadn't done him justice.

And he was a dedicated scientist who had made magic. Literally.

There were some quiet moments while Dr. Pendrake's assistant carefully hooked up the small computer system next to the podium.

Annie's mouth watered as she used the time to study the notorious Dr. Pendrake.

Easily topping six feet, his hair was dark and longer than fashionable. Today he had tied it back neatly, but there were still fiery glints shining through when he bent to straighten a cable.

His clothes were neat and well tailored, and reeked of expensively casual chic. His round-necked shirt was definitely a silk knit, and was topped by a jacket that probably had been custom made for his broad shoulders.

Tasteful khakis fell in perfect creases to his gleaming loafers.

Not a pocket protector in sight.

He stood and glanced around the audience, and Annie caught a flash of light from incredible green eyes.

Sheesh, he was sex on a stick. She dropped immediately into a fantasy of licking her tongue up the sensitive flesh just inside his very naked hipbone. And back down. And over slightly.

A tap on the microphone brought her attention back to reality, although to judge by the parted lips and squirming bodies of the few other women present, she wasn't the only one picking up the major sex vibes from this luscious set of walking hormones.

"Good evening."

His voice was as appealing as the rest of him. He should probably have a government warning stamped on his butt. Just thinking about his butt distracted Annie and she wrenched herself back to business — to take notes on the lecture for her editor.

It was a coup for her to be here, because this was very much an 'invitation-only' affair. There were some pretty impressive looking suits in the front rows, and even a military uniform or two. Her editor had sworn that this project would probably end up classified within months, and would have come himself, but his wife was due to produce a little editor any second, and he hated science anyway.

So here she was, Miss Junior Reporter, still months away from graduating with a degree in journalism, covering what promised to be *the* hot technological topic of the year — Kyle Pendrake's "Magic".

Developing a severe case of lust for the noted scientist wasn't going to help her write the feature article she'd been promised, or the spot on the front page where her byline would appear. Her palms started to sweat as she worked the first sentences in her mind...

Dr. Kyle Pendrake may have discovered magic, but in the eyes of many of his audience, he managed to create a little of his own at last night's symposium… Yeah, that would make a nice intro...oops, he was beginning his lecture.

Annie leaned forward, unwilling to miss a second of what this guy was selling. Whatever it was, she'd take some.

"Merlin." The word floated through the now-silent room like a wisp of fog. "A name synonymous with the forces of magic, the forces of nature, a command of the most fundamental elements of our existence."

The audience was hushed, all attention focused on the man at the podium. The lights struck his head and upper body, leaving much of the rest of him in shadow. A nice dramatic touch, thought Annie, and one that worked well when you looked as yummy as the good professor.

"Magic," he continued, meeting as many eyes in the audience as he could. This guy knew how to work a crowd.

"The premise that magic exists is not new. Scientists have played around with the idea for many years. At Pendrake Labs, however, we don't 'play'...we get serious!"

A quick smile moistened the panties of at least three women in the second row, judging by their reactions.

"The result of our research is here with me tonight. Ladies and gentlemen, it is my pleasure to present to you...Merlin." A wave of his hand and a click of the remote control button produced a spotlight focused on the small unit at his side. He passed his hand over it and it began to glow.

Infrared sensors, thought Annie, busily jotting down her impressions, and refusing to be seduced by the show.

"Merlin is an acronym, standing for 'Magical Energies Resonator and Linear Integration Network" board. Actually," another smile crossed his handsome face, "...it's more correctly known as M.E.R.L.I.N. dash B."

The large screen behind Dr. Pendrake lit up with the Pendrake logo and a sleek graphic of the name Merlin.

"In our labs, it's the SR388 unit, and in our system here, it's...well, it's pretty special."

A shade of excitement had crept into his voice, and Annie paused in her note taking to watch him. She could just make out a pulse beating at the base of his neck as he turned to his unit, and a faint sheen of sweat was beginning to film his forehead.

A period of very technical information followed, which Annie wisely let slip by. Her readers wouldn't care about the operating system, whether it would work on the latest PC, or MAC, how many bazillion gigs of memory it needed, or whether Microsoft would be releasing a bug update within the promised time frame.

No, her readers wanted the whole picture...the images of what she was seeing, the end result of what this machine was rumored to do.

His scientific presentation winding down, Dr. Pendrake laid his notes back onto the podium.

"You are probably all a little bit curious about MERLIN." He smiled. "We were too, when we realized what we had developed. A plug-in board that can harness every bit of magic that is lurking near it. And there is magic everywhere, ladies and gentlemen, make no mistake."

He crossed to the front of the small dais and raised the lighting in the room with another click of his remote control. He could now see his audience more clearly, and the feeling of intimacy was heightened as he swept his gaze over the forty or fifty faces that intently watched him.

Annie felt his glance like a bolt through her body. His eyes hesitated a moment as they passed over her, and she felt the pull of his attraction right down to her thong! Sheesh, what she wouldn't give for a night with this guy. No holds barred.

"There is magic in the materials we use to create our buildings, and magic in the earth they stand upon. There is magic in the plants that grow, the wind that blows, and the air we need to sustain our very lives. "

I'll just bet there's some pure magic in your shorts, too, buddy, thought Annie.

His gaze flickered back to her, and for a second Annie was aghast at the idea he might have heard her. She blushed fiercely.

"This magical energy is collected by our friend MERLIN, and converted into digital impulses. The result?"

After a suitably dramatic pause, the monitor behind Dr. Pendrake lit up with some kind of movie. There were carriages moving up and down a busy street, and people bustling about their business. But unlike old films, this one was in glowing color and the movements of the crowds were natural.

"A viewer, if you will. A glimpse through the veils of time. An opportunity to *see* the past!"

There was complete and utter silence as mouths fell open and eyes widened. Unable to believe what she was seeing, Annie was as startled as everyone else.

"Yes, you are really looking at the past. We estimate this to be New York in about 1890 or so, judging from the clothing styles. I'll leave those details to the historians amongst you — our goal is to continue to provide opportunities to peek at our past, and to learn its secrets. MERLIN is truly a magician in that respect."

A murmur rose in the room as people started to question, wonder, puzzle, and in general react in a variety of ways to the outrageous claims made by Dr. Kyle Pendrake.

"I understand your shock. Believe me, the day we first discovered these amazing results, we were pretty much in shock too. But let me assure you that this is quite genuine. These images are being generated now, here, in this room, by the Merlin system. They are not recorded, digitized, enhanced or in any other way altered. You are seeing a moment in our history — as it happened."

The murmur rose to a hubbub as the scientists in the audience started firing questions at Pendrake, the historians struggled to get their hands on pencil and paper to note what they were seeing, the military whispered to each other, and a couple of women tried to get closer to the Professor.

Annie watched it all with skeptical eyes. Could it be possible? There had been a lot of ongoing research into the nature of magic and its presence, so that had a ring of truth to it. But capturing it? Turning a computer system into a wizard? And then casting a spell to create a window on the past?

This was all sounding way too much like a bad science fiction novel. If it hadn't been for the man on the dais who was expertly fielding questions, and the images playing on the huge monitor behind him, she might well have dismissed his claims as just another hokey experiment that was designed to rip people off.

But she could see the carriages rolling along the broad street, kicking up dust from the horses' hooves. As she watched, one horse deposited a large pile of steaming droppings and a woman crossing the street behind the carriage had to do some very fancy footwork to avoid it. Now *that* was realism.

The conversations around her continued, and many people had now moved closer to the unit and the dais.

Dr. Pendrake stepped back to allow them a chance to get a good look at his system. He moved away from the crowd and stood alone for a few moments. His eyes scanned the room and found Annie.

Once again, she felt something startling in his gaze. She knew he'd looked for her this time, and was not fooled into thinking it was because he'd developed a sudden case of lust for her body.

She was pretty much used to this reaction.

Her white-blonde hair separated her from her peers on a regular basis, and her unusual violet eyes finished the job. Why *she* had been born with the genetic flaw that resulted in albinism, she had no idea, and neither had her parents. In fact, it had been several years after her birth that her pediatrician had actually realized that Annie was an albino. She had the less severe form, and her eye color was proof of that. But her hair remained obstinately platinum, her eyebrows were practically non-existent unless she used her makeup properly, and she burned to a crisp at the beach.

Her glasses took care of her minor vision problems, and it really had been no hardship after she'd learned how to deal with it.

But it still attracted attention.

Just like the attention she was now getting from Dr. Hotbody.

She raised her chin slightly and held his gaze, refusing to look embarrassed that she hadn't joined the gushing throng of salivating techno-groupies. If he wanted her attention, he was going to have to come and get it.

Always assuming that she didn't drop to her knees and offer him whatever sexual favor he wanted. It would not further her image as a cool, calm, representative of the Fourth Estate. Drooling and humping his leg was probably out, too. She sighed as he turned away, summoned by a two-star general.

It had been a nice fantasy.

Returning to their seats, the crowd settled and waited for Dr. Pendrake to conclude his presentation.

"Well, you've had a chance to take a look at Merlin and what he can do. As I mentioned to some of you, we have only looked to the nineteenth century thus far, but tonight, in honor of your presence..." he bowed politely to his audience, "...we are going to set our parameters a bit farther back. Tonight we will attempt to sneak a glimpse into the age of Shakespeare, Sir Francis Drake, and the magnificent Virgin Queen herself, Elizabeth the First."

Incredulous gasps met this announcement, and an excited buzz of conversation covered Dr. Pendrake as he adjusted settings, typed in commands, and tapped nervous fingers on the data-crystal case in front of him.

He stood, and another tense silence fell.

The monitor grew blurry and the images of Victorian New York pixilated into darkness. The room lights dipped, and for a moment nothing but the glow of the LCD screen illuminated the faces staring at it.

Then all hell broke loose. A picture appeared. It was of the ocean, and sailing upon that ocean, two enormous galleons. The picture panned around to the wharves along the oceanfront. There were sailors meandering to and fro, barrels, crates, casks and ropes piled everywhere, and women walking — in enormous gowns.

Cheers and applause and cries of surprise and wonder erupted through the conference room.

He'd done it.

Grinning from ear to ear, Kyle Pendrake also stared at the screen.

The crowd stood in unison, and Annie joined them. She was applauding as loudly as anyone and adding a couple of whistles to the cacophony. The excitement was infectious and the enthusiasm enormous.

Annie stood on a chair to watch Pendrake's reaction, and as she did, she noticed the Merlin unit next to him. It was vibrating slightly, its glow changing from a soft blue to more of an electric green. The greater the applause, the greater the change.

The size of its aura was getting larger too. Annie frowned and stopped clapping as she wondered if she should bring it to anyone's attention.

But the crowd, as the saying goes, went wild. Cheers brought out more cheers, and shouts of "Bravo" and "Magnificent" were tossed around with the applause.

The green glow was intensifying, now shining onto Pendrake's expensive khakis. There was a golden center to it, surrounding the unit, and it was pulsating. Annie realized that it was pulsating in time with the roar of the crowd.

They were the ones producing the energies that were feeding Merlin. It was eating their emotions, and liking them from the looks of it.

Little sparkles started flashing through the glow and suddenly Kyle Pendrake looked over at his creation. He froze for a second, then moved casually toward it.

God, was it going to explode?

Annie held her breath as the others continued their approbation, probably not realizing that this wasn't part of the show. The images had faded on the monitor, and the biggest source of light was now Merlin itself.

A woman, who hadn't taken her eyes off Pendrake all night, let out a loud yipping cheer, and Merlin lapped it up.

A giant fireball of light swelled around the unit, enveloping Kyle as he reached to disconnect the power.

There was a sudden hiss, followed by a screech of deafening proportions.

And Kyle Pendrake was gone...

About the author:

Sahara Kelly was transplanted from old England to New England where she now lives with her husband and teenage son. Making the transition from her historical regency novels to Romantica™ has been surprisingly easy, and now Sahara can't imagine writing anything else. She is dedicated to the premise that everybody should have fantasies.

Sahara welcomes mail from readers. You can write to her c/o Ellora's Cave Publishing at 1056 Home Ave. Akron, Ohio 44310-3502.

Why an electronic book?

We live in the Information Age—an exciting time in the history of human civilization in which technology rules supreme and continues to progress in leaps and bounds every minute of every hour of every day. For a multitude of reasons, more and more avid literary fans are opting to purchase e-books instead of paperbacks. The question to those not yet initiated to the world of electronic reading is simply: *why?*

1. *Price.* An electronic title at Ellora's Cave Publishing and Cerridwen Press runs anywhere from 40-75% less than the cover price of the <u>exact same title</u> in paperback format. Why? Cold mathematics. It is less expensive to publish an e-book than it is to publish a paperback, so the savings are passed along to the consumer.

2. *Space.* Running out of room to house your paperback books? That is one worry you will never have with electronic novels. For a low one-time cost, you can purchase a handheld computer designed specifically for e-reading purposes. Many e-readers are larger than the average handheld, giving you plenty of screen room. Better yet, hundreds of titles can be stored within your new library—a single microchip. (Please note that Ellora's Cave and Cerridwen Press does not endorse any specific brands. You can check our website at www.ellorascave.com or

www.cerridwenpress.com for customer recommendations we make available to new consumers.)

3. *Mobility.* Because your new library now consists of only a microchip, your entire cache of books can be taken with you wherever you go.

4. *Personal preferences are accounted for.* Are the words you are currently reading too small? Too large? Too...**ANNOYING**? Paperback books cannot be modified according to personal preferences, but e-books can.

5. *Instant gratification.* Is it the middle of the night and all the bookstores are closed? Are you tired of waiting days—sometimes weeks—for online and offline bookstores to ship the novels you bought? Ellora's Cave Publishing sells instantaneous downloads 24 hours a day, 7 days a week, 365 days a year. Our e-book delivery system is 100% automated, meaning your order is filled as soon as you pay for it.

Those are a few of the top reasons why electronic novels are displacing paperbacks for many an avid reader. As always, Ellora's Cave and Cerridwen Press welcomes your questions and comments. We invite you to email us at service@ellorascave.com, service@cerridwenpress.com or write to us directly at: 1056 Home Ave. Akron OH 44310-3502.

Discover for yourself why readers can't get enough of the multiple award-winning publisher Ellora's Cave. Whether you prefer e-books or paperbacks, be sure to visit EC on the web at www.ellorascave.com for an erotic reading experience that will leave you breathless.

www.ellorascave.com